THE EXCITED WARD

JENNIFER ROSE MCMAHON

Cover design by Rebecca Frank

Edited by Cynthia Shepp

Dubhdara Publishing

PRAISE FOR JENNIFER ROSE MCMAHON

"McMahon's excellent paranormal mystery. Teen and adult readers alike will be clamoring for the sequel."

— PUBLISHERS WEEKLY STARRED REVIEW

"Engaging, beautifully written scenes, and idyllic descriptions keep the tale moving at a quick pace. The characters are engaging and they draw a person in to this tale of adventure and intrigue. Adrenaline-fueled action and enough twists and turns to keep even the most astute readers on their toes, this is a captivating story with a heroine who is forcefully engaging."

— IND'TALE MAGAZINE

"As Chieftain of The O'Malley Clan I am always interested in anything to do with Granuaile, our very famous Pirate Queen ancestor. Jennifer's novel captures the connection with the past which we treasure in Ireland. The Irish landscape, contemporary social life, the Irish language, and romance are woven into this fantasy story about Maeve Grace O'Malley and her quest to solve her 'Awake Dreams'. I am certainly looking forward to the sequel. More BOHERMORE please!"

— SARAH KELLY, O'MALLEY CLAN CHIEFTAIN 2017

To those who work tirelessly at destigmatizing mental illness. Thank you for your bravery.

Remember us for we too have lived, loved and laughed.

— PLAQUE AT MEDFIELD STATE HOSPITAL

BOOK TWO ASYLUM SAVANTS SERIES

THE EXCITED WARD

by Jennifer Rose McMahon

CHAPTER 1

My shallow breathing echoed through the darkness, growing louder as I pulled on my restraints. Searing pain from the friction of the straps shot up my arms, causing me to wince. My mind chased whatever it could have been that made them think tying me down was necessary. Even if I *had* lost my mind at the cemetery—screaming with the terror of seeing my own gravestone—it still wouldn't have been enough to justify this level of barbaric treatment. As soon as they were to release me, I swore I'd sue their asses for malpractice.

Tugging at my wrist again, I hissed in pain. My skin burned like fire from the friction, and I wiggled my legs instead. My ankles screamed with the same raw sting, causing me to jump. But my shoulders lifted only a few inches before I fell from the resistance of more restraints. One push confirmed they'd strapped my hips down, too.

My heart rate shot to full panic as I searched through the gloomy darkness.

"Kaitlin? Are you there?" When my hushed voice bounced through the room, a rustle came from the far side.

"Grace?" Her voice scratched out of her.

"Shit, Kaitlin. Where are we?" I whispered. "I'm tied down. Is this some twisted form of concussion therapy, with no lights or equipment?" I stared into the blackness, listening for the sounds of nurses in the hallway.

She rustled more, whimpering in the cold shadows. "I can't move. I'm strapped to the bed too."

"All I remember is the flashing lights of the ambulance." My dry voice cracked. "And Braden's face. But that's it. They must have drugged us to calm us down when we got here."

"My wrists are sticky, and they burn," she murmured. "My straps are too tight. They're cutting into me." Her voice strained as if fighting tears.

How could they not have noticed the restraints were hurting us? The abrasive ties had injured our wrists and ankles. Someone was going to be in a lot of trouble for neglecting us when we clearly needed a much higher level of attention and care.

The blame was on our damaged heads, no doubt. Our concussions. We'd pushed ourselves too far after the car accident—to the point of being readmitted to the hospital. Again.

Unfortunately, it probably looked pretty bad this time—much worse than the other episodes. I was sure Braden had told the medics everything he saw at the asylum, particularly the hysteria at the cemetery. From what I could remember, it had included a lot of running and screaming.

I squeezed my eyes shut to remember more, picturing the abandoned asylum. Before the ambulance came, Kaitlin and I had just escaped from the boarded-up Excited Ward. It had tried to keep us prisoner inside its walls, but we'd finally broken free.

I pondered my thought for a moment. Had I just considered the ward having power to keep us inside its walls? It *did* sound crazy. But every ounce of my being believed it.

My head hurt from the effort of conjuring more of the memories of those moments at the asylum. There was panic and terror, but the discovery of the lost cemetery had made it all come crushing down on us.

Flashes of the old grave markers burst through my mind,

reminding me of the most frightening moment of my life—the reality of my own death, evidence of it.

I sucked in a gulp of air, remembering the terror that ripped at my soul as I saw my full name on the gravestone. Kaitlin's, too. And then Emma's. We'd all been there, buried beneath my feet. Together.

But how? It made no sense. I could only imagine it had to be the evil forces of the ward—its curse, messing with our minds.

Poor Braden. I thought back to his panicked reaction at the cemetery. His hands had trembled as he called 911 and his voice choked out of him in his attempts to calm me. He'd probably assumed I'd officially lost my sanity. And in that moment, I had.

But I was thinking with clarity now, with full understanding of what had happened. Too many coincidences had lined up, making the haunting events seem like more than they were. Like they were real. But I knew it couldn't be. Ghosts and cursed wards weren't a true thing.

My eyebrows scrunched together, resisting my own thoughts, like I was trying too hard to convince myself that it was all my imagination.

I wouldn't go back to the abandoned asylum though, I vowed. It was too volatile. It held too much energy. Or evil. And its truth picked at my brain. It wouldn't let us go.

"I don't want to go back there, Kaitlin. Ever," I whispered as a tear fell from my eye, trickling into my ear. My body shuddered from the memories of the sinister ward.

The more I thought about the crazy events at the asylum and the situation I now found myself in, the harder my tears fell. The salty streaks made me itch. I shook my head to help dry them, but the itch only intensified. There was nothing I could do. I couldn't reach up to scratch my own face.

"Fuck." I twitched on my cold metal bed. "What the fuck is going on? Nurse," I called. "Nurse. We're awake. We need help."

I waited for a response—footsteps, beepers, lights. Anything.

Kaitlin whimpered in her bed.

"Nurse! Help us," I yelled louder.

Finally, the sound of hard heels clomping down steps filled the space, then moved closer to the door.

"You will stop at once..." The brazen shriek of an older woman's voice blasted through the door. My breath stopped short as I listened. "Or you'll remain in The Hole for another week!"

~

My body stiffened from the cruelty in her tone. The familiar, harsh stabbing of her voice smothered my hopes that everything would be okay. And then, there was no mistake—absolutely nothing was okay.

I held my breath until her footsteps stomped away from the door before clomping back up the stairs.

"Kaitlin?" I whimpered.

But there was no answer—only the quiet sounds of crying.

"It's okay, Kaitlin. It's not real." My voice shook from the shock of hearing the woman's threat.

I didn't need to see the woman to know there was a port-wine stain on her forehead. I'd seen her before—in my flashbacks from being trapped in the boarded-up ward. Her old-fashioned nurse's cap and the glow of her rattling lantern taunted me. She'd hunted us in the Excited Ward. Tormented us with those exact same words.

"We're sleeping," I whispered. "They must have sedated us to help our brains heal. The darkness and the silence help, too."

With my reassuring words to Kaitlin, I convinced myself of our safety. I'd heard of the phenomenon before—a medically induced coma. It sounded like a big deal, but from what I remembered about our conditions at the cemetery, I honestly couldn't blame them for knocking us out for a while.

My body shook from the damp cold as I watched shapes in the room begin to take form. Dull light entered through a narrow window high on the back wall, allowing me to see shadows of details in the room. Dawn's light grew brighter by the minute, and I blinked as my eyes adjusted.

At first, I noticed the shape of the door and medical equipment by our beds. The silent monitors must have been specialized for our symptoms, with no beeping and no lights. I was grateful for the high-tech instruments, but I still didn't understand why they'd restrained us to such a high degree. Embarrassment washed over me when I considered what the medical staff must have thought when we'd first arrived—as if we were a threat to ourselves or others.

"Kaitlin, the sun's rising," I said. "We're going to be okay. Just hang on while your brain clears from whatever meds they gave us."

Her choppy breathing and sniffles were her only response. Poor Kaitlin. Terror from our predicament radiated from her.

As the morning light grew brighter, scattered streams of illumination zigzagged through the small lead-glass window, sending dusty beams throughout the room. The walls remained dark, though, and the objects within the space held their shadowy forms. Expecting the bright white and sterile stainless steel of a hospital room, I squeezed my eyes shut to reset my vision.

"Please. Please. Please," I whispered.

Please be normal when I open my eyes.

I snuck one eye open first, then the other burst wide, and stared all around the room. Damp stone walls surrounded us, dripping with moisture that ran toward a dirt floor. I gasped in horror at the unsanitary conditions, then darted my gaze toward the door. Its heavy wooden features assaulted my senses with rusted iron hardware and a lack of any window to see out.

Frozen from fear, I couldn't get my head to move as I forced my eyes sideways to see Kaitlin. My vision fell on one of the machines between us. Instead of a device displaying heart rates and respiration, it was an old wooden table that held a metal tray of needles protruding from glass vials and other old-fashioned medical supplies from at least a hundred years ago. A stack of metal bowls set on the ground, leaning on one of the legs of the table.

"What the fuck?" My voice caught in my throat as my eyes jumped to Kaitlin.

She stared at me with wild eyes as if they were about to bug out of her head. Her cheeks were sunken in, and dark circles shadowed her lids. Her grey hospital gown had bloodstains on it from the wounds on her wrists. Her restraints had cut her up bad, and her ankles showed the same level of injury.

My breath moved to panting as panic rose in me. I turned my attention to my own condition, jolting on my hard metal bed as my mind processed my own bloody wrists and ankles.

"Grace," Kaitlin whispered.

Turning to her, I felt the twisted horror plastered across my face. I couldn't hide my terror from her any longer.

"Kaitlin?"

She moved her hand, her fingers grabbing onto the edge of her gray hospital gown. As she tugged on the rough fabric, she shot me a sickening smirk.

"Grace. It's my frock." She swallowed hard. "The one from the attic in the ward. With the 'M' on it."

CHAPTER 2

Appalled, I stared at Kaitlin's gray frock before glancing at my own. Screams threatened to tear out of me, and I stifled them with the meager remains of my inner strength.

It had to still be a dream. A nightmare.

An ambulance had taken me away from the frantic scene at the cemetery, Braden by my side. But where was he now? And where was my mother? And Kaitlin's parents?

We were alone.

Abandoned.

I prayed for swift rescue from the lunacy of my dream. To wake up lucid and to be normal again. But even my grip on the details of what I hoped for started to fade. I struggled to keep Braden's face fresh in my mind, but he blurred and blended into a sea of strange faces.

It began to feel like what I had been hoping for, the reality I craved, was the actual dream. This, here and now, was my new reality.

"Kaitlin. What happened?" I whispered. "How did we get here?"

Her eyes remained fixed on me, unblinking.

"We shouldn't have tried to escape again," she murmured. "It's impossible to escape this place."

Her words caused my focus to narrow into a fine point of clear sight. Understanding washed over me, widening my eyes with the clarity I'd been avoiding.

We were patients here.

Trapped against our wills in this place of darkness and doom.

The ward had won. It held us within its walls.

We were prisoners in the Excited Ward of the Blackwood Insane Asylum.

"Do you remember anything?" I asked. "Do you remember the…" I thought hard to recall the details of my memory. "The…"

"I remember screaming," Kaitlin said. "I remember running. And…" She strained to find words.

We had both lost hold of the clouded events that landed us in this place. I glanced at the tray of needles, knowing I would do anything to ensure they didn't administer any more of whatever had been in them.

Obedience.

That was what they sought.

Compliance.

It was all they wanted in a place like this, so we would have to give it to them.

"We need to do whatever they say," I whispered. "If we fight, they'll give us more medicine."

She nodded with a choppy motion.

"Don't even complain about the straps," I added. "We can take care of our wounds ourselves. We just need to get out of here before we die of hypothermia or starvation." Pausing, I strained to hear beyond our door. "We just need to be patient. And wait."

Kaitlin rustled on her bed, shifting her hips to the side. I felt it, too —the ache in my bones from the hard surface of the cold slabs we laid on.

She turned her head toward me again. In a low tone, barely audible, she asked, "Where's Emma?"

Kaitlin's words exploded my mind into shattered pieces that scattered out of my reach. Hearing Emma's name evoked a level of emotion I couldn't contain. Fear and desperation burst out of me in a flood of tears with loud gasps for life-saving air. The sound of my erratic breathing filled the room, escalating the tension to heights of sheer panic.

"Water therapy?" I squeaked.

I barely hissed the words, fear that speaking them would make them true. Could they have sent Emma for more water therapy?

"I hope the hell not," Kaitlin answered. "She barely survived the last time they tried to drown her."

Jesus. Emma always got the worst of it. Nurse Totten hated her for some reason. Her spirit. Her intelligence. Her beauty. Those natural blessings all worked against her in this place.

"Nurse Totten." I spoke her name out loud with a shudder.

I was sure she was the one who'd shouted at us through the door. And she was the one who would have tortured Emma, too. Totten had no soul. Her empty eyes held only vacant hate. Someone must have hurt her at some point, and she was determined to get vengeance on those weaker than herself.

"You mean Nurse Rotten," Kaitlin murmured. "Her birthmark gets brighter every time she gets mad. Its purplish shade is the perfect measure for how much trouble you're in." Her weak smirk pulled up one side of her face. "So do we just wait for her to come back for us?"

I thought about our other options. We could find a way to unfasten the straps, push our beds to the small window, and break out of it somehow. But then what? Disoriented and probably drugged, we could get lost and then caught again. Our punishment would be even worse the next time. Worse like Emma's.

"I think we just wait," I said. "It's the only way to get to Emma. If we run now, it would be like leaving her to the wolves."

"You're right." Kaitlin dropped her head back onto the metal slab with a bang. "How did we even get caught? I can't remember any of what happened."

No matter how hard I searched my memory, I couldn't find the pieces of what occurred either. Whatever drug they gave us, it had caused full-blown amnesia. It felt like we had brain damage.

"I'm not even sure what happened before all of this." I groaned. "Like, how did we get sent to a madhouse in the first place?" My entire existence was a blur, and I stared at the needles and vials on the tray, as if they were to blame. "But at least I still feel like myself, you know, smart, resourceful. Like I know I can outthink Totten. We can figure a way out of here. We just need to be clever and keep our wits about us."

The calculating clarity in my brain gave me certain confidence we wouldn't rot in here. I believed deep within my soul we had what it took to get out. We just needed the chance.

"How do we outsmart them when they're the ones with the keys and the power?"

"We'll trick them," I stated. "We need to act scared. And submissive. Like their punishment worked, and we're ready to be compliant. That's all they want. They just want us to be mindless zombies."

Kaitlin drew in a deep breath. "Okay. But how the hell will we convince Emma to do it, too? She's way too headstrong and outspoken."

Chuckling, I said, "I know."

Just thinking of Emma's antics made me laugh. She never put up with anyone's bullshit, and she was ready at all times for whatever confrontation was ahead of her. It was her downfall, though, in a place like this. From the moment she'd set foot here, she'd known she was doomed.

"Wait," Kaitlin shushed me. "I hear someone coming."

My heart jumped into my throat as I listened. Kaitlin was right. Someone was moving around outside of our room, maybe more than one person.

I gathered my composure, preparing for whoever might walk through our door. No matter how hard I tried, I still nearly lost continence from the terror.

Turning to Kaitlin, I barely made a sound and whispered. She stared at my mouth, reading my lips while straining to hear me.

"We need to be compliant. Be agreeable to whatever they ask. No matter how embarrassing or shameful it may be."

She nodded.

I continued, "They will violate us. They'll treat us like animals. But we have to be grateful for their kindness. Do you understand?"

Kaitlin gulped as if trying to swallow a basketball before nodding again.

Before I could say anything else, the door smashed open with a crash.

Nurse Totten stormed in first, followed by a smaller-framed nursemaid who peered at us from behind her. Light poured into the room from the hall, and I squinted against its assault.

"What a shame. Light too bright?" Nurse Totten chided.

My first instinct was to sneer and roll my eyes. Instead, I averted my gaze to avoid confrontation, determined to keep a solemn expression on my face.

Totten turned to the nursemaid behind her. "Unfasten the restraints. They'll need to relieve themselves." Her callous voice cut into my flesh like the crack of a whip.

The meek nursemaid came to my bed first, then fumbled with the straps. Her eyes met mine as she loosened them from my bloody wrists, and a flash of pity crossed her face before she could shield it.

I allowed my freed wrists to remain at my sides even though the urge to rub them and move my arms at that point was unbearable.

She removed the other restraints that held my body to the metal slab, and I nearly leaped out of my skin as the joy of freedom coursed through me. Instead, I remained still and barely moved a muscle.

The nursemaid shifted to Kaitlin next, and I kept watch over Nurse Totten from the corner of my eye. She stared at me, assessing my condition, then hesitated like she wasn't sure what to do next.

"Up for yer piss," she barked as she kicked a metal pan across the floor toward my bed.

I sat up, then quickly hopped off the metal table while keeping my

11

eyes off the purple mark throbbing on her head. My knees wobbled beneath me, and I held the edge of the bed for stability. Shivers quaked through my entire body as I positioned myself over the pan.

Shyness over peeing tested me under these circumstances, and I grimaced as my bladder muscles tightened like a vice. Squatting, I hovered over the pan while holding the fabric of my frock up around me. Under Nurse Totten's stern glare, I was certain I wouldn't produce a drop. Fortunately, my attention shifted to Kaitlin. The horrified expression painted across her face sent a jolt of laughter through me.

Her eyes nearly fell out of her head at the sight of me hovering over the pan, then, in my efforts to stifle my laughter, my pee released. I hid my reddening face in my chest in hopes they would think I was crying instead of laughing. And all I could think about was how I was going to kill Kaitlin for hitting my funny bone at the worst possible time, yet again.

As soon as I was able, I lifted my face and finished. I dreaded Kaitlin having to go through the same humiliating process as Nurse Totten kicked a pan toward her next.

"I'm sure you'll enjoy your breakfast," she said as she gestured for the nursemaid to bring in the tray.

Now was my chance to take attention off Kaitlin so she could do her business with a little privacy.

"Yes. Thank you," I said in a low tone with my eyes locked on the floor. "Where should I bring this?" I asked, reaching for my filled bedpan.

Nurse Totten stood taller with her shoulders squared. "Bring it to Agnes. She'll show you what to do with it." She glanced at my bloodied hands and feet, then looked away in disgust.

I lifted my pan carefully, taking small steps with it, not only to avoid sloshing, but also to allow time for Kaitlin to finish and follow me. Agnes had us spill the contents into a vessel on her cart, then we went back into our room without any argument or hesitation.

I climbed onto my bed, signaling for Kaitlin to do the same. With a few adjustments, I prepared for the restraints again.

"Eat yer breakfast first," Nurse Totten barked.

"Thank you," I said as I reached for the tin bowl of curdled porridge.

Kaitlin followed my lead. We ate the cold, clumpy mush like it was a stack of hot, syrupy pancakes. In a few gulps, we were scraping the bottoms clean.

"Thank you," Kaitlin murmured.

"Speak up, Missy," Nurse Totten grumbled. "No mumbling."

"Thank you," Kaitlin said with more power. "Thank you for the nice breakfast."

Her eyes dropped, the last syllable nearly choking her, but I was proud. She was doing great.

We both adjusted on our beds, preparing to be restrained.

Nurse Totten paced, as if deciding what to do. Then, after what felt like an eternity, she stepped out the door.

"They're ready to come up," she shouted.

CHAPTER 3

K eeping silent, I stared at Kaitlin in exhilaration at our imminent release. There was no telling how long we'd been in this room, but the weakness in my legs proved it was at least several days, if not more.

"Don't speak of this place with the other girls," Totten growled. "Not a mention or you'll find yourselves back in here for a longer stint. Agnes will see that you get cleaned up before you reenter the ward." She clomped her way along the damp hall, adjusting her white cap as she led us to a set of dark stone stairs.

At the top was a sealed wooden door. We were in the basement of our ward—appropriately named 'The Hole'. No one could hear the forgotten girls down here.

Nurse Totten pushed on the door, loosening its seal, then pivoted to us. "Have no mind of trying to run away again. We won't stand for you giving the other girls notions of what might exist out of these walls. It only causes anxiety and upset to their structured time here." She pushed on the door one final time, and it groaned open. "Consequences for disturbing the order of the asylum can be severe."

Agnes followed us, carrying the tray from breakfast. She avoided eye contact at all cost, and it exposed her vulnerability. It was clear she was new here, a nurse-in-training maybe, and her heart hadn't turned to stone yet. At least there were still a *few* humans left in this place.

Nurse Totten ushered us along a hallway on the first floor, then led us into a small room with Agnes. A low, wide tub full of water sat in the middle of the room.

"Get them cleaned up and return them to their hall," Nurse Totten ordered Agnes. "No delay." Then she turned and rattled her hard heels down the corridor.

Kaitlin and I moved to the tub in an instant, dying to wash the dried blood and filth from our bodies and hair. We whipped off our frocks, and I lifted my toe in first. My foot retracted—almost feeling as if the freezing water electrocuted me.

My eyes darted to Kaitlin's, and she pressed her lips together in resignation. I stepped into the freezing water, and she followed. Ladles and old bars of soap sat on a bench next to the barrel, and we wasted no time pouring gray water over ourselves. Our bodies shuddered from the cold, but we moved quickly, finding joy in the simplicity of getting clean.

Agnes handed us ripped towels that felt like they must have once been sheets, and we did our best to dry off with them. Bending, I wrapped the fabric around my hair and then flipped it back like a turban. Agnes stared like she'd never seen such a thing before, and I nearly laughed at her confused expression.

Kaitlin watched Agnes' baffled reaction, letting out a small snort from holding her own laughter in. I nearly lost it. My shoulders shook, and I used all my mental power to think of something else, something sad, so I wouldn't burst out laughing.

It was crazy. Even in a place like this, the deep connection Kaitlin and I felt allowed us to find humor under even the most oppressive conditions.

"Okay, come on," Agnes urged. "Up to your rooms."

We followed her through the whitewashed halls and up a flight of stairs. She opened a heavy metal door, then walked with us down a long corridor.

"You're to be separated now," she said. "Each with a different room. Nurse Totten's orders."

My eyes darted to Kaitlin's. Separation wasn't an option. We needed as much time together as possible to conspire our escape. But challenging Nurse Totten's orders was the last thing we could do at this point.

"You're here." Agnes pointed me to my room. "And you're there." She aimed her hand to the tiny room across the hall for Kaitlin. "Now, do as you're told and there shouldn't be any trouble."

Her words warned us, and I tucked it away in my brain. I stepped away from my door as Agnes began closing it. Kaitlin stepped deeper into her room, too, trying to hide the look of fear in her eyes. I nodded to her, trying to convey, "It will be okay. We are safe here."

But I knew better. We were far from safe.

As my door clicked shut, I stepped closer to its cross-shaped window and peered across to Kaitlin. Her face filled her window as well. Glancing up at the marker over her door, I studied it. Its familiarity poked at me, as if trying to remind me of something important. It held the numbers '235,' and I wondered what their significance could be.

Then, as I dropped my eyes back to Kaitlin's, motion in the window of the door next to hers caught my attention. A face pressed against the glass, staring across at me. She moved up and down as if bouncing from excitement. Then her voice burst through to us, filling the hallway. My heart skipped a beat, and I jumped with happiness. At the same time, I lifted my finger to my mouth to shush her.

But she still yelled for us.

"Finally! Jesus Christ," she screeched. "What the hell did they do to you? You look like shit!"

Her voice echoed through the hall, and I prayed Nurse Totten wasn't in earshot.

Kaitlin raised an eyebrow in disbelief, waiting for a confirmation. Without hesitation, I gave it to her.

I mouthed, "It's Emma!"

~

My natural instinct was to get to Emma and shut her up before the wrath of Nurse Rotten was upon us again. I jiggled the handle of my door, intending to sneak across to her, but found it locked from the outside. My heart rate quadrupled, and beads of sweat formed on my brow as the walls closed in on me.

Trapped.

Isolated.

Solitary confinement. It was barbaric and probably illegal. If I could only contact my family… or anyone who cared about me. I just couldn't remember them yet. Whatever the staff had done to me in The Hole still had my brain fried.

"What'd the wench do to you?" Emma yelled into her little window, pressing her lips to it.

I lifted my finger to my mouth to shush her again. "We're okay. It doesn't matter now. We just need to get off their shit list and back to normal."

Emma reeled back from her door in laughter, then called again. "You come up with the craziest words. Shit list! I love it. A list. Of shit. And we're on it." She coughed, and the maniacal smile on her face fell. "Back to normal? What does that even mean?"

"It just means if we follow the rules, we get some of our freedoms back," I yelled. "So we can all be together again. That has to be our focus."

When I looked across at Kaitlin, her eyes flew wide as the sound of clomping echoed across the tile floor. I shot a glance to Emma, drawing my hand across my neck to stifle her. She sneered at me.

The footsteps silenced for a moment, then slowly walked the length of the corridor. I fell away from the window, then sat in the corner of my small cell. A shadow passed across the door, darkening the space for a moment, before moving on.

Room checks. Their interruptions were frequent and violating in their own way—never knowing when someone would peek in, which broke our concentration and removed all sense of privacy. It was another piece of the torture sequence. Stealing away at our independence. Our identity.

The footsteps moved on, then faded into the next wing. Our three faces popped back into our windows immediately.

I lifted my finger to my lips, waiting for a nod of agreement from them. Kaitlin and Emma agreed to the silence, and we waited for our release.

It could have been twenty minutes—or it could have been six days. It was impossible to measure time in solitary. Just staring at the white walls closing in around me sent my mind into a panic of isolation. The only thing to do was go crazy in my own whirling thoughts.

Flashes of faces. Running. Confusion. People calling my name.

Pieces of information taunted me like a broken sequence, leaving me with no ability to put them back together in the right order.

But besides the flashbacks, I had a feeling in my gut. Those were the parts I could trust. Someone always told me, "Trust your gut," and it was the right thing.

My gut told me I was strong. It told me I was smart. And it told me I was going to get out of this place and make a life for myself.

But then my head took over, allowing fear to reenter. And insecurity. It was then I began to lose hope.

The walls crushed in closer, and my breathing accelerated. The room was running out of oxygen, and I struggled with shallow gulps. Sweat beaded on my forearms, and the room began to spin. I crawled toward the door, certain I would pass out any second, but kept my eye on the open space between the bottom of the door and the floor. It was my only hope at getting air.

Scenes in my head accelerated to the point of nearly exploding my mind. Sounds intensified with voices and banging that made me reach for my skull to keep it from shattering.

And just as a scream built in my throat, preparing to screech out of me, my door flew open. Fresh air and bright light spilled over me, and I pushed onto my knees to allow it to wash over me.

"You'll join the others for dinner." A harsh voice grated on my sensitive ears. "I expect perfect behavior. Not a single step out of line. From any of you."

My gaze lifted from the black shoes, then moved across the apron of her stiff uniform. Avoiding her face, I looked past her to see Kaitlin and Emma emerging from their rooms.

Relief moved through me like warm honey, and I stepped out of my prison in elated silence. We lined up behind Nurse Totten, silently following her out of solitary and into the bustle of the rest of the ward.

I'd nearly lost my mind in my small prison cell, and I shuddered at the thought of ever having to go back in there.

But now—now I was out. And I was with my friends. This moment was precious, and I needed to protect it with every ounce of my being.

"All in line," Nurse Totten commanded. Her voice caused a wave of girls to scramble out of their rooms.

They struggled to keep their excitement contained when they saw us. A few waved and giggled. Others rocked and grinned. Some just bounced like little children.

Their greeting was a beautiful thing, and it filled my heart up. Several of these women, young and old, belonged here, needing full care and assistance for disorders, but others, like us, had been broken over the years and lost their will to be who they were once meant to be. I prayed that would never happen to us.

I vowed, actually, to never let it.

A line of gray frocks moved through the building, then exited through a side door. The ease of leaving the locked building confused me. Maybe it was because I had been in The Hole and solitary for so long, but it seemed like more—like the doors to this ward had the power to control me, to keep me within their walls. Forever.

We walked down the cobbled path out onto a gravelly paved road. Kaitlin slowed her pace to end up alongside me with her shoulder nearly touching mine, while Emma bounced ahead with her face tilted upward, soaking in the warm rays from the sun.

I looked across at all the red brick buildings of the institute, and their windows reflected the light in every direction. Bright white paint on the moldings of the entryways surrounded large black doors leading to different wards. It reminded me of the Wellesley College campus, which I'd previously visited. I must have been considering college at one point. But then something derailed me.

My gaze landed on the chapel, running along its stained-glass windows. Tilting my head up, I noticed the high tower that displayed a huge clock face. It read 4:30. But in this place, time mattered little.

A strange banging drew my attention away. Over and over, like the rhythm of a hammer, the banging pounded through my chest. The girls in our line continued walking toward the dining hall without a flinch, but Kaitlin and I slowed, swinging our heads toward the sound.

High fencing surrounded a concrete courtyard housing a pole on one side with a wicker basket nailed to the top. I searched within the fencing, then landed on a figure standing by the pole. It was a boy.

He stopped bouncing his ball, staring in our direction. Probably the same age as we were, somewhere around nineteen or twenty, he was tall with his hair cut short around the sides and a bit longer in the front. His sweatshirt said, 'Springfield College'.

My stomach flipped from the surprise of seeing a young man among my existence of all women. But in the same moment, it clamped tight and I froze. He stood without motion, his gaze hollow. The ball in his hand dropped to the ground, then bounced away from his feet. He didn't flinch, but only kept staring with a glare of warning, like he was unsafe. Or dangerous.

I pulled on Kaitlin's arm, moving with the line of girls again.

"Did you see him?" I whispered.

"Yeah. He's creepy," she said.

I turned back for one more look before whipping my head front again. He was still watching me with his dead-eyed stare.

"Shit," I mumbled.

Emma fell back to us with a smirk. Her head shook as she read the expression on my face.

"You saw Bobby?" she asked, eyes on the fenced court.

"You know his name?" My eyes widened.

"Ya. Of course. Everyone does," she said. "He's the one who was in all the papers. You know. The psycho."

"I don't remember."

"Shit. What'd they do to you in The Hole, Grace?" Emma teased. "They freakin' wiped you clean."

She was right. The darkness of The Hole still trapped me. Whatever treatment they'd done to me had affected my memory. I prayed it would come back with a little time.

"Why's he in that fencing? All alone?" I peeked one more time as we entered the dining hall, noticing a guard by the gate.

"Maximum security. They keep him in Ward B," Emma said. "You know. The one with the high fences and guards roaming the boundaries. I think they keep him on suicide watch on the triage floor. No one can figure him out yet."

We filed into the dining hall, then sat at one of the long wooden tables. Each of the five tables had at least twelve chairs, all facing in the same direction—toward a higher, more formally set table where the staff sat.

They'd given us stew, a roll, and a spoon. One glimpse at the staff's table showed me their options were more diverse and prepared with special care.

I took my spoon and stirred the liquidy stew, finding one small piece of beef amongst the soggy carrots and potatoes.

"Are you insane!" Emma swatted at my hand. "Wait for grace, Grace." She giggled.

A moment later, the room awoke with a chant-like prayer, offering thanks for the food in a sickening monotone. After the final word, I turned to Emma again.

"What did he do to get in there?"

Kaitlin leaned in and stared at Emma, waiting for her reply.

"Well now, don't get all judgy about it," Emma whispered. "But they say he murdered his parents."

"What?" Kaitlin stopped chewing and stared.

Dropping my spoon, I waited for more information.

"Yeah," Emma continued. "They say he put a hammer through the back of his father's head, then stabbed his mother multiple times in the kitchen. He jumped off the high cliff at the quarry after, but he somehow survived the fall."

"Holy shit," I mumbled.

I was shocked. His handsome face and athletic build had told a different story, one of a promising college athlete, but the look in his eye—that was the dead giveaway. There was something sinister brewing within him. Something…off.

"He looks kind of crazy," Kaitlin said with a sneer.

"Well, he doesn't think so," Emma added.

I shot my gaze back to her. "What do you mean?"

"He says he didn't do it. Says he has no memory of the events." She shrugged her shoulders. "No one knows what to believe."

My throat tightened as my appetite shrunk away. Everyone in this place had a story. Not everyone truly belonged here. Many had disabilities requiring the care of an institution, but others were held as prisoners against their will—punished for conditions unexplained or misunderstood.

And we knew who we were.

And this boy was one of us.

"I wonder what he's like," I mumbled.

"Well, I bet he's a good kisser," Emma blurted. "Did you see those plump lips?" She pulled in close to us and whispered. "We should meet him."

My eyes darted up to make sure no one heard her. Guilt oozed from my stare as I perused the dining area, landing directly on Nurse Totten. She glared back at me with a scowl, and I quickly pulled my eyes away from hers.

"If Rotten ever catches us talking to him, we'd be dead meat," I stated through clenched teeth.

Emma shrugged her shoulders. "I'm dead, anyway."

CHAPTER 4

E mma's words of death haunted my mind. Her rhetorical response of being 'dead anyway' must have referred to her situation of being imprisoned at the asylum, but it somehow still frightened me—like a prophecy from deep within her soul.

As we walked back to our ward, I wondered why she was even held in a place like this. She seemed so...normal. Then I searched my memory for clues about how *I'd* ended up here, I found none. My gaze landed on a lone building, and I stared at its familiar entryway. A sign above the door said, "Administration,' and I assumed it must have been the first building I'd entered here. Intake procedures were performed--completing my paperwork, determining my condition and my needs, selecting which ward I'd be confined to.

A flashy automobile boasted from the shade at the front of the Admin building—regal and stately, like something a wealthy person would own—probably the superintendent's motor car. Its spoked tires held thick white rims, and a fabric canopy roof topped its body. The front grill propped two large globe headlights. For some reason, the modern vehicle looked like an antique to me, like something seen in a museum. But it was clear, at the same time, that it was the latest model, shiny and new.

I pinched the space between my eyes, swiveling to Emma. "Don't make fun of me, but…what year is it?" I asked.

She looked at me like I was nuts, but then her face turned serious. "It's 1920, baby. The best of times." She ruffled my hair before turning away.

Inhaling a deep breath, I held it. I knew it was 1920. I didn't know why I had to ask, but it just seemed like I needed to be sure. A strange feeling of time and place left me unsettled, like something was off. And I knew it was the lingering effects of The Hole, but I felt trapped in a time warp.

"Don't worry," she added. "Time is different when you're held prisoner. It can move forward. It can move backward. Or not at all. It just stands still. You get used to it."

"It feels…." I hesitated, looking around again. "It feels like it's moving side to side, off its rails. And it's fragile. Like it could break at any moment."

"Huh?" She pulled her attention away from the court to me.

"Nothing." I searched for Bobby, too, but he was gone.

Maybe I didn't want to know the truth of how I got here. Maybe that was why I couldn't remember. It might be my mind's way of protecting me, sheltering me from something unpleasant. Avoidance and selective memory were coping mechanisms that were proving to be quite effective.

I studied the girls who filed into the Excited Ward—some with messy hair, others pulling at their lashes or flicking at the air, and many talking animatedly to themselves or just staring off into oblivion. Kaitlin, Emma, and I were different though. We were awake. Alert. And together, we were an unseen force. There was a connected power between us I felt deep within me.

So the decision was mine. I could continue to exist here, following the rules and biding my time to see what would become of me. Or I could dig in, uncover the truth hidden within these walls, and fight to reclaim my life. All *three* of our lives.

I'd made the decision the moment I awoke in The Hole. I had just been avoiding it from fear of further punishment or of learning something I wouldn't be able to handle. But I knew my destiny, and it included finding answers. Taking charge of my life. And getting the hell out of here.

It was the point of no return.

Energy returned to my spirit, and I stood taller. Intricate plans wove through my mind as I formulated my next steps.

"I need to find my file," I whispered. "Where do they keep the medical records?"

Emma's eyes grew wide with intrigue.

"Now there's my girl, come back to life," she said. "I've been waiting for you."

I turned to Kaitlin as we moved down the corridor of the ward with the other girls, headed to the art room.

"We need to see what they're saying about us," I whispered. "Like... why we're here and how they've diagnosed us."

"We'll get in so much trouble, Grace," Kaitlin whined. "We'll get caught." She rubbed her sore wrists.

I instinctively touched my own wrists, then raised an eyebrow at Emma. "Do you know where the files might be?"

"We can start in the shrink's office," she said with a smug grin. "That creep writes everything down. Whatever he wants. Making us look like loons." She paused. "When all he really wants to do is fuck us."

A shudder ran through me. I knew exactly what she was talking about, only she was brave enough to actually speak it. It was just a feeling from the ward's psychiatrist, the kind I got when someone looked at me a certain way, and I instinctually knew what they were thinking. We couldn't trust him. His bad intentions oozed from his every wanton glance.

"How can we get into his office?" I asked Emma.

"The orderlies have keys. They go in and out emptying trash and shit." She paused in thought. "I bet I could get Patrick to let us in. He's always staring at us, but he's sweet enough."

Entering the art room, I surveyed the easels and canvases set all around and moved for the ones furthest away. We settled into three stations next to the back window, then lifted our brushes.

"That's insane," Kaitlin whispered. "He's one of *them*. He'll tell on you. We'll get caught somehow."

"Doubt it," Emma replied. "He's a puppy dog. Probably looking for his first girlfriend."

I glanced around to be sure no one was listening. "So, when?"

"If we can stay out of solitary and get back in our regular rooms, then we can sneak out after final room checks." She pointed at our easels. "So paint a fucking great picture. Sunshine and daisies and shit. Make 'em think you're as stable as a faithful church-going spinster."

Kaitlin blotted a big yellow splotch onto her canvas, held her brush in place, and mumbled, "We're gonna hang for this."

Kaitlin was right. There was no telling what they would do to us if we were caught breaking into the medical office. But we had to do it. It was the only way to get the information on our backgrounds—information Kaitlin and I needed in order to understand who we were and how we got there.

"I know exactly what my file says." Emma sat back, inspecting her progress on her painting. "It's got big words and heavy labels, all for the same thing—*girl likes boys too much*." She laughed. "Everyone's so prudish. As soon as a girl shows interest in a boy, she's a whore. God forbid she likes sex. Ooh..." Her hands wiggled in the air for emphasis. "Well, I don't buy it. If men can enjoy sex, then so can we." She paused. "I was just born in the wrong century. That's all."

It was true. Emma was a modern woman. We all were. Our thoughts were bigger and broader than the women around us. We didn't live by the conformist rules set by society. We wanted independence. Power. Equality.

Yet, we only received punishment for seeking it.

It was no different a hundred years ago when they were burning strong women at the stake. I was certain the women who burned were the ones who pushed against the rules. They weren't witches at all. They were the ones who showed resistance and stood up to the patriarchal society. The men cowered from the thought of a woman having an opinion or showing knowledge or mastery of a higher discipline. They had to suppress them for fear of having to call them equal. Instead, they called them witches and hags. Burned them alive.

A century later, so-called witches weren't publicly burned anymore. But rather, we were clinically diagnosed—imprisoned against our wills and given modern labels of mental illness and instability.

It was crap.

And it was time to push back against the archaic system of suppression.

I studied my painting, hoping it would demonstrate mental stability and compliance to those who were so eager to judge me. Instead of smears of dark purple and black storm clouds that yearned to come from my brush, it depicted green trees and white clouds with a golden sun in the corner of the canvas. Seemed perfectly appropriate to me as a means of disguising my true mental condition. Rage.

Glancing at Kaitlin's work, I observed blotches of colorful petals and leaves, like a festive bouquet of flowers. She had the right idea. Then, when I peeked at Emma's, my hands flew up and covered my eyes as my face reddened. I dragged my fingers down my face in response to her blatant disregard for giving two-shits about what anyone thought of her.

A single flower filled her canvas, like an orchid. Its numerous ivory folds drew the eye into the bright red center. A thick stem poked toward the middle of the flower as if preparing to thrust into it.

"Jesus, Emma!" I gasped. "You'll be strapped with a chastity belt if you're not careful."

"It's just a flower, Grace," Emma chided. "Get your filthy mind out of the gutter. Jeez. It's not my problem what people choose to see in my floral artwork. That's on them."

I turned away from her painting, not wanting to stare. It elicited an internal response in my belly that only true art could, and I didn't want to admit the lustful fantasy it evoked in me. But then my eyes smacked right into Betty's—a nice woman from our hall. She blinked, pulling her gaze away from Emma's painting as if caught with her hand in the cookie jar. But it was too late. I'd already seen her blank stare and open mouth. There was still life within her somewhere, and the painting had stirred it up for her too.

"It's good. Isn't it?" I said to Betty.

She nodded. "Uh-huh." Then she dropped her blushing face lower and stared at her hands.

I wondered what had landed *her* in the asylum. She appeared relatively normal. Middle-aged. But fragile. Something must have happened to her at some point. Something she couldn't get over.

My throat constricted with sympathy for her. She could be a mother. Someone's wife. But instead, they'd trapped her here. I reached across, touched her arm and smiled, trying to comfort her in some way, but then my attention snapped back.

"That's it, ladies," a voice called from the door. "Time to clean up and get settled for the night."

We scurried to tidy our stations, always avoiding the wrath of being last. Placing our brushes in cups of water by the sink and hanging our smocks on the coat hooks, we kept pace with the others. As we moved toward the door to leave, I guardedly glimpsed in the direction of solitary.

But the stoic nursemaid motioned her hand in the other direction. "You three are to return to your rooms tonight. Keep out of trouble for a change. All you need to do is follow the rules. It's that simple."

I glanced down the corridor for any sign of Nurse Totten, praying she'd gone back to the nurses' quarters at the far side of campus for the night.

"We will," I told the nurse. "No need to worry about us."

Emma snuck up behind me. "Quiet as church mice." She shot a sinister grin at the nurse.

I jabbed her in the ribs with my elbow.

∾

My stiff mattress and metal bed frame had never been more inviting and comfortable. I didn't even mind the overcrowding of six beds squeezed into a space intended for four. Instead of one in each corner, we were in rows of three, taking up every available inch. Kaitlin and Emma had separate rooms with their own set of problems, including similar overcrowding, but in the moment, I was focusing on my own situation and how I would navigate it. They'd have to do the same if we were to execute our plan.

The girl next to me cried quietly in her bed. It was normal though. She cried all night—every night. The one next to her picked incessantly at her nails, leaving only bloody stubs at the end of each finger. Another mumbled to herself and turned away every time I glanced at her. The final two in the room acted like no one else existed in the entire world. They had their own realities and none of us were a part of them in any way. I laid quietly on my bed, waiting for Emma's signal.

An almost-full moon passed across the window, glowing off the chipped-paint panes, and I kept time by its motion. Heavy breathing around me proved the others were asleep, and the lull of the rhythm weighed on my own lids. Images of the clock face on the chapel tower whirled in my mind. Then, a sense of deep fear filled me, and my heart accelerated. Distant screams filled the dark corners of my thoughts, and my eyes flew open. I blinked into the sound of gentle tapping, only to realize I'd fallen asleep and had been dreaming.

When the tapping continued, I sprang out of bed, breathless.

Emma.

On tiptoe, I wove through the maze of beds and made it to the door, quiet as a mouse. Gripping the handle, I turned it with a gentle motion until it unhinged. I eased it open just enough to slip through.

"What the hell? I thought you chickened out," Emma whispered with a sneer.

"Sorry. I fell asleep," I said as I closed the door behind me. "I'm exhausted."

It was only then I realized how much my body craved rest. I hadn't slept properly in The Hole for who knew how long, and I seriously needed to recover from that trauma.

She pulled me along the corridor past the other doors.

"What about Kaitlin?" I slowed.

"She wouldn't wake up. No surprise," Emma replied. "I tapped her door first. Sound asleep. Basically, she's scared shitless."

I wasn't surprised either. It was amazing *I* even woke at all. It was probably because of the disturbing screaming in my dream. Cries of madness that unhinged me. It was just as well I'd been woken. Anything was better than hearing those terrifying sounds ever again.

"We need to go up to the third floor. To solitary," Emma said. "This way."

My body stiffened from the idea of going anywhere near solitary. I shuffled my feet as if it would slow me down, avoiding the inevitable. But the third floor was where the shrink's office was, so we had no choice. I clenched my fists and followed Emma to the stairwell.

"How will we get in? Did you find Patrick?" I whispered.

"No sign of him. But I didn't want to lose this opportunity to check things out," she said. "We can at least try to get in on our own."

"What about the night nurse?" My voice shook. "If she catches us, we're dead."

"No shit. That's why she won't catch us." Emma reached into the pocket of her frock, then pulled out two pairs of stockings. She handed one to me. "Pull this over your hair. You can cover your face with it if someone comes."

"Like a criminal?" I stared at the stockings in my hand.

"If the shoe fits." She smirked as she pulled the opening of the stockings onto her hair.

The disguises offered a false sense of security, but it was better than nothing.

"How often does she come around?" I glanced up the stairs as we started climbing.

"Sometimes often. Sometimes never. Depends if she falls asleep at the nurses' station or not." Emma bit off a nail and spat it out. She reached for the door leading to the third floor, then opened it in slow motion. She popped her head in, swiveling to see both directions. "Coast is clear."

I followed right behind her, stepping on the backs of her heels, as we entered the quiet wing. My eyes moved down the corridor and landed on the archway hiding the doctor's office door. The memory of an old wheelchair flashed in my mind, and a ghostly feeling chilled me from the inside.

It was late. And it was dark out. My nerves had been thoroughly shot over the past few days. I wasn't sure if I had it in me to go any farther.

An echo thumped in the back of my brain. A familiar pounding. And my senses clicked into high alert.

"I don't think I can do this," I whispered, hearing the banging rhythm growing louder.

"We can't turn back now," Emma pressed. "Come on."

We shimmied down the length of the corridor, and I refused to look into the cross-shaped windows of any of the solitary cells. Even as I passed the exact one the wardens had kept me in, I forced my gaze to remain forward. As we passed under the archway at the end of the hall, I turned my head to the left, knowing the alcove behind the arch hid the medical office door.

The fogged glass panel in the wooden door said, "Medical Office". Smaller words beneath it read, "Staff Only".

My breath sucked in as Emma reached for the tarnished brass doorknob. It clicked as she turned it in each direction, but it didn't turn fully. *Locked.*

"Dang it," she mumbled as she fumbled all around for a ledge or a mat, searching for a hidden key.

The pounding continued in the back of my mind, and I turned to the stairwell just beyond the office. This stairwell was at the opposite end of the wing, set on the front side of the building instead of the back. I crept to the opening of the stairs, then peeked in. There was a window at the lower landing.

"This way," I whispered and moved into the stairway, following the sound of the banging.

I jumped down the stairs to the window, then lifted up on my toes to see out.

There, across the road near the dining hall, was the boy—Bobby—bouncing his basketball and shooting it toward the peach basket with only the glow of a lantern for lighting.

Emma joined me at the window.

"Hello, lover," she purred. "Fancy seeing you here."

Then my attention whipped behind us as a voice cried out from the solitary wing.

"What's that pounding in my head," a voice shrieked from one of the cells. "Pounding! Pounding! Pounding!" A maniacal laugh followed her repetition as she lost her mind to the torture of it.

"Dorothy," a heinous voice barked. "You will be silent, or you'll be kept in there another week."

My eyes shot wide with terror.

"Shit! It's Totten!"

CHAPTER 5

We flew down the stairs, back to the second floor, certain Totten was on our tails—her hot breath stinking up the back of my neck. My feet slid across the tiled floor as I slowed at the door to my room and grabbed the handle.

I glanced down the hall to be sure they hadn't seen us. Emma's finger lifted to her lips as she warned me not to make a sound. With a nod, I opened my door in silence as she snuck away toward her room.

Climbing into bed with my breath racing in and out of me, I squeezed my eyes shut to help reduce the squeaking of the metal frame. I pulled the itchy wool blanket over me, then my breath caught in my throat.

"Where were you?" Through her sniffles, Jeannie's baby voice slapped me in the back of the head, and I choked on my own spit.

With suppressed coughs, I struggled to reply before she said another word.

"Bathroom," I hacked.

"That was a long time," she whispered, sucking in small gulps of air from her continuous crying. "Aren't you afraid of the dark?"

Her innocent eyes widened as she hugged her teddy bear closer. Since she usually just cried all night, I was stunned to see her attention redirected at *me* instead. Judging by her full figure and considerable height, I'd always guessed she must be at least my age, if not older —but was contradictorily childlike.

"Nah. The dark's okay," I assured her. "But I'm scared of other things. I think everyone is afraid of something. Don't you?"

"I'm afraid of the dark," she whimpered.

"I know. I'm sorry." I reached for my pillow, then passed it to her. "Here. Hug this. With your bear in the middle. Darkness is the pillow's favorite. Its true purpose comes to life in the nighttime. It will help you feel safe, and you'll feel its joy if you try."

"Really?" She reached for the pillow, then placed her bear between it and her belly.

"Now squeeze."

Smiling, she hugged the pillow.

"You'll be safe now," I said with a grin.

She leaned slightly out of her bed and held her eyes on me. "What are *you* afraid of?"

Her words tore straight into my soul, exposing my vulnerabilities with every syllable. Totten. The Hole. Solitary. These were all things I was afraid of. But there was one thing that terrified me beyond all others. One thing that I feared beyond words.

Myself.

My true identity.

How I ended up here.

These were the things that frightened me most.

"Spiders," I stated, then rolled over.

As my eyes closed, my erratic thoughts drifted back to the medical office door and how I would open it. That door was the direct link to my deepest fears, I now realized. Though I had no choice but to face it head on. And getting my hands on the key was the only way. I'd heard the jangling of keys at the nurses' station a million times and ignored it, but now…now it was all I heard in my mind.

My eyes flickered open from the rays of dawn's light entering the room. My exhaustion had taken me over, and I'd slept more soundly than I had in my entire life. But the bliss of waking flushed out of my skull as soon as my reality came crashing in. The fleeting moment of serenity wasn't lost, though. It teased me cruelly, even in its short life. But it gave me something to hope for.

Then I remembered the details of my truth. I was a prisoner. Abandoned in an asylum for lunatics. Discarded by the unwell people around me. But the ethereal echo of rattling keys resonated in my ears, and my focus sharpened.

Before long, the sound of the morning bell for room checks and breakfast broke my concentration. I made my bed, then pulled my hair back with a string. Glancing over at Jeannie, I caught her fluffing the pillow I gave her before she tucked her bear under it for safekeeping. Her pajamas and lace-trimmed underwear were typically kept under her own pillow, but today, they were neatly set to the side.

As I stepped into the corridor, I searched the crowd of girls until my eyes landed on Kaitlin. We hurried together down the hall to the common room, and I searched around for Emma. She usually sat on the couch by the transistor radio, fiddling with the controls on the carved walnut panel, hunting for reception other than men speaking of the war. Any time she found any form of jazz, she'd turn it up, making the place feel like a roaring nightclub. Of course, the nurses always made her dial it down, but the few simple moments of loud dance hall music transported us to a place shared with socialites and bachelors.

But Emma wasn't in her spot by the radio.

We searched through the sea of gray frocks, then snuck back to Emma's room to peek inside. Empty.

She was gone.

My hand went to my mouth as I stared at Kaitlin.

"Maybe she got caught," I murmured.

Kaitlin froze. "Did you guys sneak out last night?"

I remembered Emma scampering down the hall after leaving me at my room in the middle of the night. We'd made it back safely from our trek to the medical office, but maybe she never made it back to her own room after that.

"Yes. We tried to wake you, but…"

"Jesus." Kaitlin's panicked voice nearly stopped my heart. "That was too risky. Now where is she?"

My worry for Emma's whereabouts shot terror through me. Could she have been caught? But how? Last I knew, we'd made it back to our hall before anyone saw us. I strained to understand what could have happened to her.

With our hearts in our throats, we spent the day searching for Emma. Nurse Totten detected it, too. Her evil glare oozed pleasure every time she caught me looking around for my friend. But she knew something more. She had Emma. Her side-eye stare and tapping foot proved she'd get *me* next, too.

By dinner, I couldn't deny it any further.

Emma was in The Hole.

My gut twisted as I thought about Emma trapped in The Hole. Alone. Scared.

Everything within me shifted, my only focus now was on saving her.

Getting my hands on the keys had suddenly become a matter of life and death.

Kaitlin and I finished our dinners quietly, and her nervous jitters were like a flashing sign we were up to no good.

"Just act normal, Kaitlin," I mumbled into my burnt bread roll. "You're freaking me out."

Her knees bounced under the table. "I'm trying, but Rotten keeps glaring at us."

"She's just trying to intimidate us. Don't look at her. Ever." I fought the urge to focus on the staff table. They were probably all in on it, thinking submission was the only way to control us. "I'm going to find her tonight."

Kaitlin coughed, crumbs flying out of her mouth. "What?"

"I have to." I placed my spoonful of soup near my mouth to hide my lips. "She could seriously go crazy down there. Or even die from the cold or whatever else they might do to her. It's not an option to leave her there alone."

"Grace. If you get caught…"

"I know." I dropped my spoon as my appetite vanished. "It won't be good." My primal fears of brutal punishment threatened to redirect my planning but then the sound of rhythmic banging pulled my attention toward the door. "We have to get out of here, Kaitlin. Seriously. Before they kill us all."

"Rise!"

I jolted, standing without hesitation as the dining staff barked the command.

"Bowls to the rear!"

Everyone lifted their dinnerware, then carried it to the counter at the back for cleaning. We moved to the door, and a nurse led us out in single file.

Keeping our eyes down to avoid the nurse's glares, my urge to look up grew with each pounding bounce.

Bobby was in his fenced-in court. Bouncing his basketball, over and over. From the corner of my eye, I glanced his way. His silhouette stood at the edge of the fencing, facing us, and the bouncing grew stronger and louder.

I couldn't resist the temptation any longer, and I lifted my eyes.

Instantly, his gaze grabbed mine and didn't let go. He slowed the bouncing of the ball as if waiting for information from me. One of his shoulders lifted slightly, then he glanced around me as if searching for someone. His eyes landed back on mine, and I understood. He was looking for Emma.

I closed my lids and shook my head slightly, letting him know it wasn't good.

He dropped his ball, and it rolled away from his feet. Then continued to watch us as we filed back to the Excited Ward.

Determination washed through my veins. I had to get to Emma. It was up to me now.

"I need your help to make a distraction," I said to Kaitlin. "Just long enough for me to get a peek in the nurses' station. To find the location of the keys."

"Christ." Kaitlin closed her eyes.

"I knew you'd be eager to help." My chipper tone mocked her, knowing she hated the idea, but she would do it.

Kaitlin was afraid of so much, yet she was also very brave. Her nervous nature made her appear to be a coward, but I always knew I could count on her. She faced her fears in private and I caught glimpse of it in her eyes, every time.

We entered the side door of the ward with the other girls, then climbed the stairway to the second floor. I watched the night nurse as she shuffled into the 'staff only' area and I peered in behind her. At first glance, I saw white smocks hanging on hooks at the side and silver trays stacked along the back counter. A wooden cabinet with glass doors held bottles and trinkets on its shelves. I'd have to get inside the station to see more.

I glanced back for any sign of Nurse Totten, then turned to Kaitlin. "Now," I whispered.

Her eyes flew wide, but then she took a step back as if preparing to execute her plan.

A second later, she started retching. Strange gurgling sounds escaped from her throat as if she were choking.

"She's going to throw up," one of the girls screamed, retreating in disgust.

Kaitlin leaned over, stumbling away from the station. Making gagging sounds, she reached for her throat.

The night nurse flew out of the station, rattling a trash can in her hands. As she got closer, Kaitlin fell to her knees, scrambling even farther away.

Struggling to hide my smile, I held my breath to keep from laughing out loud at her overly theatrical antics. I turned my focus on the open nurses' station, looked for any witnesses, and slipped in. Everyone's attention was on Kaitlin's episode and whether she would live through her convulsions. I only had a matter of seconds to scour the room for what I needed.

I searched every wall hook and surface, but I found nothing. My heart pounded in my ears, warning me to get out of there as quickly as possible. Instead, I continued my mission and rummaged through the space. A desk at the front of the room held papers and pens. A wooden box sat at the edge. I darted for it, then lifted the cover. Inside was a metal ring with several keys of various sizes hanging from it.

My breath sucked in as my heart exploded in my ears.

Now was my chance. But was it too early in the evening? Would the nurse need them before lights out?

I couldn't risk losing the opportunity, so I grabbed them. Once I dropped them into the front pocket of my frock, I stepped out of the doorway back into the corridor.

My vision blurred from the panic coursing through me, and I struggled to follow the chaos in the hallway.

Kaitlin was still on all fours. The nurse held her shoulders, saying, "Let it out. Don't hold it in."

I moved into the crowd of girls, blending into the group of ogling spectators, then inched into Kaitlin's view. I dropped lower to catch her eyes. In one quick glance, she realized I'd completed my task.

Her retching slowed, and she sat on her heels, blinking into everyone's faces.

"Are you okay?" the nurse asked.

"I think so," Kaitlin whispered, holding her stomach. "I think I need to lie down now."

"Yes. This way." With a look of confusion on her face, the nurse helped Kaitlin stand, ushering her toward her room.

A second nursemaid entered the hall, calling to all of us. "This way, ladies. Music time."

Jeannie bounced up and down, clapping her hands. "My favorite," she squealed.

Music time. *Ugh, welcome to hell.*

The sudden shift from my stealth espionage to the mundane exercise of banging on instruments none of us knew how to play gave me mental whiplash. I closed my eyes and rolled them in private.

The music room was across the hall from the art room, and I was convinced they were both there to covertly torture us. Not a single one of the girls was musically inclined, yet the staff still believed the activity to be therapeutic. Finger cymbals, bongo drums, and rhythm sticks kept them all busy, while out-of-tune guitar strumming tormented my ears.

But in this moment, it was perfect. I would use the chaotic distraction to my benefit. I entered the room with the others, hiding the heinous grimace that threatened to cover my face. Perusing the boxes of instruments, I reached for a shaker and rattled it back and forth as I moved around the room, blending into the gray maze of other girls.

A mute patient who usually just grunted a lot got carried away with her drum, per usual, and pounded on it with growing angst. Most eyes moved to her, awaiting the inevitable head banging that typically came next. As the irritating drumming and strumming continued to agitate the room, I inched my way back toward the door, appearing lost in the blending rhythms of the random noises. Then I slipped out.

Sneaking away from the bustle of the agitated activity, I slid into the stairwell, out of sight. With each unauthorized step, I planned my excuses and reasons for being off my floor, in case I was caught. None seemed good enough, but I kept moving anyway. I snuck out onto the first floor, darting my gaze down the hall. I remembered the general direction of the heavy door to the cold basement, but I was hazy on the details.

Keeping my wits about me, I followed my intuition and moved toward the backside of the building. A dark narrow alcove drew me closer. And there, hidden at the rear corner, was the ominous door.

I stared at it, wondering why it agreed to hold such frightening secrets within its seal. Terror filled every part of me as I stepped closer. If I entered and it slammed behind me, locking itself, I'd be trapped. Then caught. My skin bristled with nerves on high alert.

Then the sound of clomping heels filled the space behind me. And voices.

With no other options, I ran to the door, pulled it open, and snuck inside without making a sound.

∾

With my hand still on the latch, I held my breath and listened. Silence filled the space around me, and I slowly released the door handle. The glow of a single light hanging from the ceiling cast gentle illumination around the damp, dark walls. I moved down the stone stairs, trailing my gaze alongside the narrow cellar space at two doors along the edge.

I reached my hand into my frock, then wrapped my fingers around the keys. Careful to not make a sound, I pulled the keys out and stepped closer to the first door. The metal handle had a large keyhole beneath it, and I checked the keyring for the one to fit it. A sizable skeleton key stood out prominently from the others with its long shaft and square notched bit. Wiggling the key into the opening, I twisted.

Resistance within the lock kept the key from moving at first, but as I added more pressure, a mechanism within shifted. I grabbed the knob, then turned it. The latch popped open, and I pushed the door inward.

My heart pounded in my ears, blocking out all other sounds and disrupting my other senses. My muscles tightened as I attempted to look inside. With a deep breath, I leaned in and blinked as my eyes adjusted to the darkness.

Pale evening light shone in gray streaks from a high window at the back. The room was empty except for a row of floor-to-ceiling rectangular boxes stacked against the back wall. My attention drawn to the details on the boxes as I stepped farther in. Handles, latches, and name tags covered the front of each case—some heavy canvas, others leather. Suitcases.

The compacted lives of each girl in this prison. Their identities, hidden away in a forgotten place.

My eyes widened in wonder as I searched for one I might recognize. My own.

I considered what might be in each of the patients' suitcases--the items they'd packed and brought with them, assuming they were here only for a short visit. My stomach clamped, causing sickness to rise in my throat, knowing there would be no end date for most of them. The suitcases were part of the farce to get them here in the first place. Then a sound jolted my head back toward the other door.

I stepped out of the storage room and closed the door, then jumped to the other one. My hand trembled as I jiggled the key into the lock. I glanced behind me, trailing up the stairs I'd come down to be sure no one had followed me. Then the lock clunked, and I twisted the knob.

Pushing the door open, I peered into the black of the room.

"Fucking bitch," a voice slurred out of the darkness. "You'll burn for this."

"Emma?" I whispered into the dank space.

"Jesus! Grace? Is that you?" Her voice rose in decibels. "Get me the fuck out of here!"

I scurried into the room, following the sound of her voice. My eyes adjusted to land on the metal slab bed they'd once tied me to. This time, they'd restrained Emma there.

"Oh my God, Emma." I reached for the straps on her ankles, then fumbled with the fasteners. Her feet were cold as ice. "What did she do to you?"

Her body shivered from the cold, and I squeezed her arm to feel her temperature. She had no blankets. I inspected her more closely, eyes rounding at her nakedness.

"What the hell, Emma? Where are your clothes? You'll freeze to death." My voice cracked in horror.

"Fucking Rotten took them. Probably went all lesbian at the sight of my body." She grabbed my hand. "She says she'll freeze the hot lust out of me."

"What the hell does that mean?" I yanked my hand, needing to undo her restraints.

"She caught me last night when I snuck out to see Bobby."

I gasped. "You snuck out? Oh my God! Are you crazy!"

I froze in disbelief. She'd actually left the ward in the middle of the night. To see the psycho-killer. I pulled on her restraints again, trying to loosen them enough to return circulation to her feet. With a full inhale, I remembered who I was dealing with. It was Emma. Of course she would sneak out to see him. And I couldn't blame her. There was something very alluring about him.

I snapped my attention back to her straps. "I need to get you out of here, Emma. This just isn't right. It can't be legal."

"No, stop, Grace. You'll get in trouble." She squeezed my hand to stop me. "I have to stay here, or they'll know you freed me. We can make a plan to escape once I'm out of this dungeon."

"But you'll freeze to death," I whispered. "I need to get you a blanket."

"I'll make it until morning. And when she checks on me, I'll be sweet as a princess. I promise." She clenched her muscles to generate body heat. "If I'm not back by lunch, then, yeah, a blanket would be good. And maybe a hatchet to assist me in my great escape." She chuffed. "Now get out of here. Don't get caught."

"I don't want to leave you." My voice shook.

"It's okay. I'm much better now that I know you know where I am." She squeezed my hand again. "How did you get the key?"

"I stole it from the nurses' station." My voice stuck in my throat, desperate to find a way to rescue her.

"Are there other keys with it?" she asked.

"Yeah. A bunch." I looked at the door where they hung from the lock.

"There must be one to the medical office," she said. "Use it. Now! Don't lose this opportunity. Open that fucking door and look at our files. Tonight!"

CHAPTER 6

I couldn't just leave Emma in The Hole all night to freeze. But getting a blanket and sneaking back in was too risky. I had to return to the music room before they noticed I was missing.

"Go," Emma urged.

My feet resisted moving to the door, my eyes remaining glued to Emma's eyes.

"Wait." I turned to the door. "I have an idea. I'll be back in two seconds."

After I crept out of the room, I moved to the door hiding the stacks of suitcases. I pushed the door open, then entered the storage room. When I pulled one of the cases from the top, a cardboard name tag swatted my face. I lowered the suitcase to the floor, inspecting the writing on the tag. The darkness of the room made it almost impossible to read, but I was able to make out the name 'Elizabeth Miller'. Maybe this was Betty's.

I snapped the side fasteners, and the case popped open. Propping the lid against the tower of suitcases behind it, I reached in and felt around for clothing. Small boxes, picture frames, and a perfume bottle sat on top of layers of fabric. I pushed the trinkets aside, then pulled out the first item of heavy wool. With one shake, it fell open in my hands. A navy-blue peacoat, as long as a dress, with shiny brass buttons running down the front on both sides and a smooth silk lining. Betty would want me to use it for Emma. I had no doubt.

I ran back to Emma, then draped the coat over her.

"Oh my God. Thank you." Her voice cracked. "But when Rotten comes back in the morning..."

"I'll come back at dawn and put it away," I said. "Are your restraints okay? Do I need to loosen them more?"

"No, I'm okay. Just go," she said.

"I'll be back. I promise."

I wiggled the keys out of the lock. The only way to return to Emma at dawn was if I left it unlocked. I had to return the keys right away, before they missed them, and there was no way I'd be able to steal them a second time in the same night. I could only pray they wouldn't notice the unlocked handle when they came for her in the morning.

"Grace?"

I paused before closing the door. "Yeah?"

"You're a..." She swallowed. "I mean, I don't know what would have happened if..." She hesitated again.

"It's okay, Emma," I said, nodding with understanding. "We need to stick together. To help each other. That's what friends do. Now try to get some sleep."

"Thank you, Grace," she whispered as I closed the door with a click.

I secured the door to the suitcase room too, though leaving it unlocked as well, then headed for the cold stone stairs. My heart raced in my chest as I climbed two stairs at a time. I put my ear to the heavy wooden door at the top. No sound of clomping heels or hushed voices, so I opened it as quietly as possible and stuck my head out.

My mission was to get back to the second floor, undetected, then figured out my next steps from there. If anyone stopped me, I'd have to pretend I was ill or delirious. But if Nurse Totten found me, the gig was up.

I snuck out of the dark alcove hiding the basement door, then moved toward the stairwell. The sound of a closing door snapped my attention in the opposite direction, and I froze against the wall, listening. I shimmied along the hard surface, sneaking a peek through an archway opening into a grand foyer area. Dark wood molding and an oriental carpet near the large front door of the ward staged a false sense of elegance that soured my stomach.

My breath sucked in as I stared at a family who'd just entered. A husband and wife, both dressed to the nines with fancy hats and expensive clothing, their daughter cowering behind them as two nurses in white uniforms approached them. The late evening hour proved the family was making a rash decision, one based on emotion rather than logic, and they'd soon regret their impulsivity.

Grateful for the distraction, I bolted for the stairwell and flew up the steps in huge leaps. I couldn't help but think about what I'd just seen though. That family had no idea what they were doing. Part of me wanted to race back and tell them to turn around, take their daughter back, and run. They probably thought they were doing the right thing, getting help for their cherished child. Instead, they were signing off on her death sentence.

I hesitated at the door leading to the second floor. The sounds of echoing drumbeats and clanging cymbals traveled out to me. The activities in the music room continued in full swing. No one missed me. I pressed my hands on the door, ready to push and return to the safe space.

But then I paused and thought about the new girl again. I wondered what they'd write in *her* file. How they would manipulate *her* life now. And I remembered…

I had more to do.

Taking my hands off the door, I turned and raced to the third floor. Pushing the door open, I looked down the corridor for any sign of staff. The hall was quiet, and I ran past the narrow doors with cross-shaped windows, praying no one was inside any of them. When I reached the archway at the far end, I stopped at the door to the medical office. Pulling the keys from my pocket, I fumbled with them, searching for one that might fit the lock. My trembling hands could hardly feel the cold metal in my fingers, and I dropped the keys. A loud rattling clang bounced through the hall, and I froze.

Within a second, I had the keys back in my hands, this time with more confidence. I pushed a key into the small opening at the knob. It stuck, so I tried another. The third key slid in, and I turned it. A clunk within the housing vibrated through my hand, and my eyes widened. I pulled the key out, certain it had down its job.

Clomping sounds from down the hall pulled my attention away, and I straightened my spine. I jumped to the stairwell by the office and hid within it. Peering out to check if it was all clear, I pulled back from the sight of a white uniform moving down the corridor. Pivoting, I sailed down the stairs back to the second floor.

The continued sound of music filled my soul with hope, and I ran toward it. My mind raced with panic, blurring my vision, as I tore down the hall.

The nurse's station came into view as I got closer. Approaching it, I prayed I'd be able to return the keys to the box before anyone knew they were even gone. Just as I slowed to peer into the station, a white uniform filled its doorway and stepped in front of me, blocking my entry.

My gaze lifted, meeting her steely eyes. My heart plummeted to my feet as I stared into her evil, twisted face.

"What are you doing out of the music room?" Her gruff tone hit me square in the face. A blur of purple darkened her brow, sending terror through me.

With my mind shattered into a million shards, I stared, speechless, into the sinister eyes of Nurse Totten.

My hand flew over my mouth by instinct, as if to stop her words from reaching me—or maybe to stop myself from saying anything that would land me in The Hole.

I puffed out my cheeks against my hand, like trying to suppress vomit. I immediately recalled Kaitlin's antics and their effectiveness.

"I think I might have a sour stomach. I didn't want to upset the girls in the music room." I glanced back toward the strumming and clanging, as if I'd just come from there. Then I burped into my palm, widening my eyes in panic.

"For the love o' Christ," Nurse Totten bellowed, turning on her heels into the nurses' station. "Wait for the bucket."

I followed her in silence. While she reached for the trash bin, I flipped open the wooden box on the desk and dropped the keys in with a jerk. The sound of my fumbling made her snap around. I straightened, hiding the box behind me. My uncontrollable trembling launched me forward, falling into Nurse Totten, adding to my feigned condition. She shoved at me to avoid getting my sickness on her, and I stumbled back toward the door.

"Out of the station. You know you're not allowed in here," she shouted.

I fell out of the room like a delirious drunkard and leaned over, holding my stomach. She tossed the trash can in front of me before quickly retreating.

After one more retch, I let out a huge belch.

"Oh, that's better." I sighed. "I think I'm okay now. I just need to sit." I shuffled toward the sound of the music, holding my stomach for extra measure, then shot into the room out of her sight.

My body twitched with spasms of adrenaline and dissipating panic. I'd escaped Rotten and returned the keys, all at the same time. It was a miracle and my collapsing body rippled from the strain of it.

"What happened?" Kaitlin was by my side in two leaps.

"I found Emma," I whispered. "She's in The Hole."

"Is she okay?" she begged.

"She's better now that she knows she not forgotten." I glanced around the room, certain all eyes would be on us, but everyone continued to remain focused on their instruments.

"Did anyone see you?" she pressed.

"I don't think so." I thought for a moment. "Maybe the new girl. But that's it."

"What new girl?" Kaitlin stepped even closer.

"Some new girl was being checked in on the first floor." I remembered her lost, frightened gaze. I could tell she felt it—the ominous hold of the ward, but she but had no idea the hell it would truly become for her.

"But no staff saw you?"

"No. Except Rotten." My eyes flew wide. "She nearly caught me when I went to return the keys."

"Shit! Grace!" She seethed. "If you get caught. Or any of us. I swear, she'll kill us and say it was an accident."

She was absolutely right. Totten had no soul. She never flinched when a patient died. It was as if she saw it only as a reduction in her workload. A bonus.

"She's trying to kill Emma." I nodded. I thought of Emma freezing, naked in The Hole. If I hadn't given her the coat, there was no telling what would have become of her.

Kaitlin's jaw fell lower and lower as I told her the details of my mission. She jumped at every scary part.

"I can't believe you were able to unlock the shrink's office, too," she whispered.

"I can't either, actually. Emma would've killed me if I didn't." My head dropped to the side as finger cymbals clanged repeatedly, piercing through my brain. "I have to sneak back in there later tonight," I said in a hushed tone. "And I need to get to Emma again before sunup. To hide the peacoat."

Kaitlin's head dropped, and she moaned. "No... I can't handle the stress. This is crazy."

"No, what's truly crazy is Emma went out of the ward last night."

"She tried to escape?" Kaitlin bit at her nails.

"No. She snuck out to meet Bobby at the court." I whispered.

"What," she blasted through clenched teeth to keep as hushed as possible. "She met him?"

"Yup." I smirked. "We'll get more details once she's out. But judging by the sly smile that crept up her face when she told me, I think she likes him…a lot."

She closed her eyes, pressing them with her fingers. "We're never getting out of here," she mumbled. "There's just no way."

As I laid flat on my back in bed, I regretted giving Jeannie my only pillow. My head pounded from the remnants of the deafening music room compositions, and I made ocean sounds in the back of my throat to drown out the residual clanging of cymbals on my eardrums. But my annoying ailments were actually welcomed, as they kept me awake and ready to make a move for the medical office when the time was right.

"Check." The night nurse opened our door, blinding me with the light from the hallway, counted heads, then shut it.

Now I just had to wait for everyone to fall asleep.

I stared at the small panes of the window as rain hit it and rolled down. The chipped paint and ominous shadows of night sent a haunting sensation tickling down my spine. I shook it off before it could settle too deeply within me, knocking me off my plan of action.

Soon, slow, heavy breathing all around gave me the assurance my roommates were asleep, so I slipped out of my bed. Barefoot, I snuck across the room in silence and opened the door. With the stealth of a mouse, I exited and scurried down the hallway toward the stairwell.

The door to the nurses' station was open, and I turned to look inside as I passed it. I'd fake sickness again if caught, but I needed to know if the night nurse was still out on walkabout.

As I peered into the station, my eyes landed on her feet. With legs splayed outward, she slumped across the chair. Her jaw hung open, and small snores vibrated her nostrils. It was my best chance at getting this done while she slept—hopefully for a long time.

I snuck into the stairwell, then climbed to the third floor. Stepping through the door, I glanced both ways before bolting toward the medical office. A dull glow of a lamp hanging from a cord above helped illuminate my path as I hurried along.

The bottoms of my feet smacked against the tile with every stride, then I slid to a stop at the shrink's door. I reached for the handle, praying it was still unlocked, and turned it. The knob jolted in my hand as it moved the bolt out of its housing, then popped the door open.

A gasp escaped my lips and I snuck in, closing the door behind me in an instant. If I was ever caught in here, there was no telling what the punishment might be. Breaking and entering into a doctor's office was by far the most real offense I'd ever done here. But there was no turning back now. I needed information on how I got sent to this heinous place. And for my friends too. If we were ever to get out of here, we needed to know who we were. Pressing my back against the door, I caught my breath in an attempt to slow my racing heart.

Subtle light of night entered the windows at the rear, illuminating the office furniture. I felt around on the desk for a lamp, running my hand up its stem to find the chain. When I tugged on it, a buzzing glow came to life within its green-glass shade.

In two quick strides, I was at the oak file cabinet flipping through metal-edged hanging folders. Hand-scrawled labels stuck up from the tightly packed files, and I leaned in closer to read them. Names. Last names, followed by first, and my fingers flew through the alphabet to the Ps.

Parker, Grace

I tugged the file out of the drawer, then plopped it under the gentle glow of the desk lamp. Handwritten notes shifted within. I pushed them aside, revealing the Medical Sheet. My breath stopped short as I skimmed the words as quickly as possible.

Fall from running horse. Delirium. Brain fever. Melancholia. Disappointed expectations.

I'd been injured. Thrown from a running horse. Brain trauma.

But my diagnoses sounded ridiculous. Brain fever? What the hell was that? Disappointed expectations? Basically, I had a head injury followed by sadness, probably a result of the abrupt set back in life.

And it got me sent here. Now they twisted it to make it look like I had mental illness. My teeth strained under the pressure of my clenched jaw.

I read the notes under the diagnosis statement.

Father passed. Mother unable to care for her. High level of resistance at sectioning to Excited Ward.

So I fought back when they sent me here. The idea of my resistance frightened me. I must have sensed the injustice all around me. Or worse. I likely felt the evil from the soul of this place. I still felt it, all around me.

Below the notes were the doctor's prescriptives.

Restraints for excitability. Hydrotherapy for brain fever. Seclusion for calming.

Unbelievable.

My eyes jumped to the door as terror began to spill over. I shouldn't be here. The diagnoses were ludicrous. I was old enough to take care of myself. My 'melancholia' and 'disappointed expectations' were a goddamn part of growing up. And with a brain injury, of course it would all be heightened. Jesus.

I rubbed my head as the pounding increased. Being thrown from a horse would certainly explain my headaches. And maybe even my strange feelings of deja vu. Brain injury was no joke and it clearly impacted me more than I could have realized.

I shut my file, then rifled through to grab the next one.

Edwards, Kaitlin

Kaitlin's Medical Sheet was on top. I drew my finger down the page to the diagnoses.

Congestion of brain. Quackery. Hit to the head.

Scribbles on the side of the page said, *nervous nature, possible suppression of menses.*

My teeth ground together. How dare they? Being sent to this place was violation enough, but then to have a strange man make decisions about a woman's condition, a condition he had no idea about, was maddening. But then I focused back on Kaitlin's diagnosis again. She had a brain injury, too. It probably explained why we understood each other so well, and basically connected the moment we met. Quackery, they called it.

Other words like *requiring full care, institutionalized for own benefit, parents couldn't cope*, filled the margins. Complete bullshit.

I shifted my attention to her prescriptives.

Restraints for excitability. Hydrotherapy for quackery. Seclusion for calming.

The exact same as mine. Her assignment to the Excited Ward made it clear—her treatment, and all other patients too, would be the same, no matter the condition.

My eyes darted toward the door again, half expecting it to burst open with loud accusations and damnation. But I fought my urge to run. Instead, I shoved Kaitlin's file back and grabbed the next one.

Grangley, Emma

My hands trembled as I carried it to the desk. Her file was heavier than ours were, and I hesitated to open it for what I might find.

As I opened the folder, words jumped off an array of note-covered papers. *Hostile. Irrational. Disconnected. Antisocial personality. Lack of Empathy*. There were a variety of terms that sounded nothing like Emma. Sure, she was opinionated and strong-willed, but that wasn't illness, nor was it punishable. Or was it?

I pushed the scraps of paper aside to uncover her Medical Sheet.

Her diagnoses read, *Immoral life. Seduction and disappointment. Psychopathy. Nymphomania. Self-abuse.*

My head shook in disbelief. A liberated woman who could think for herself—punished. Imprisoned.

They just wanted us all to be compliant puppy dogs in this society of men. As soon as a woman showed any independence, opinion, or power, men exiled them. Excommunicated them. Extinguished them. Rage heated my face.

Lower on the page, I read her prescriptives. *Restraints for hysterics. Hydrotherapy to cool the lust. Seclusion for calming.*

Figured.

But there was more. Additional comments filled the small space below the original prescriptives. *Insulin therapy—temporarily effec-*

tive but short-lived. Shock therapy—effective for sedation but short-lived.

Oh my God. They were experimenting on her. There was no way those treatments could be helpful, or even safe. If anything, the procedures would only subdue her by frying her brain to mush.

Then my heart stopped as I read the last words.

Candidate for orbital lobotomy.

CHAPTER 7

My mind exploded with terror causing my vision to blur. Our medical records were worse than I could have imagined. They'd created terms and conditions that were typical personality traits and twisted them into mental disorders and deviance.

And now, they planned to turn Emma into a drooling corpse. Just because she was an open-minded, strong-willed, independent woman. The world just wasn't ready for her. But I idolized her for it. She wasn't afraid of anything or anybody. She just blazed her trail the way she wanted.

But I had to warn her. I had to tell her what the doctor was suggesting for her next treatment option.

It was malpractice, clear as day. If anyone were crazy, it was the shrink. His misinformed judgment came from a place of misogyny and intimidation. He couldn't handle her strength, and the power she wielded over him. It was obvious Emma was sane. Sure, her energy and enthusiasm might be off-putting to some, but imprisoning her for it was ludicrous. And now they were planning on killing her. Maybe not in the full sense of the term, but making her brain dead through a barbaric lobotomy was the same thing.

I slammed her file shut as my teeth ground together, but then I heard a distant bang. A clang. Then, the rattling of metal in the hall. My heart jumped into my throat, and I reached for chain of the lamp. With a whack, my hand smashed into the glass shade, nearly knocking the lamp off the desk. I launched to catch it before crashing to the floor, but ended up creating more knocking as I settled it back on the desk. Holding it firmly in place, I stared at the door, certain it would burst open any second.

Holding my breath, I reached up the shaft of the lamp and pulled the cord to turn it off. With a click, all went dark, and I waited in silence with my eyes wide open.

After a few moments, I released my breath in a long exhale and crept to the file cabinet. Returning Emma's folder, I gently closed the drawer and left the oak cabinet as I had originally found it. A fleeting moment of disappointment ran through me, the craving to read Betty and Jeannie's files pulling at me. And maybe even the new girl's file was somewhere around here. Their histories and the causes of why they'd been sent here gnawed at me. But now, my only focus was escaping this office and getting to Emma.

I snuck to the office door, then put my ear on the etched-glass window. Silence returned to me from the other side, so I turned the knob. The click of the mechanism echoed through my bones, causing my hair to stand on end. I waited another moment before pulling it open.

Peering out through the crack, I listened and watched for any shadows, then snuck out into the hall, closing the door behind me. I ran straight for the stairwell with the stealth of a gazelle, then leapt down the first flight. As I turned to take the second set, I reeled back in horror as a dark figure blocked my way. Unable to stop myself in time, I barreled right into them and we fell into the side wall.

Terror at my imminent capture surged through me, a scream building in my throat. My first instinct was to struggle and escape, but strong arms held me steady, and my only recourse was to keep my face hidden. I kept my head down as I pushed against them.

"Whoa. Slow down." His voice soothed me. "Where are you going so fast?"

I pushed off his chest to create distance, staring into his face. Patrick. The orderly. Thank God.

"Please don't tell anyone," I begged. "They'll punish me."

"You're supposed to be in your room," he replied.

"I know. I had a nightmare. I just needed to get out of my room for a minute." I retreated to put distance between us and pressed against the railing behind me. "Can you just pretend you didn't see me? Please."

He nodded. "Sure. Yeah. No problem." He smiled gently. "Are you gonna be okay?"

His concern confused me. Instantly, tears sprang to my eyes at the unfamiliar compassion.

He reached for my shoulder. "Whoa. It's okay," he said. "I didn't mean to upset you."

Then the tears poured, and my shoulders shook with sobs. He froze, staring at me as if not sure what to do, but still, I couldn't stop.

Rubbing my shoulder awkwardly, he said, "I'm sorry. Please. What can I do to help?"

I sniffled. "Why are you being nice to me? Everyone in here is always so awful."

Moving back slightly, he stood straighter. "I-I don't know. I guess I can just tell which of you don't actually belong here. And it makes me mad."

My crying stopped as I pulled in new air. "What?"

"Yeah, it's obvious," he said. "You and your friends. It's just not right."

My mind exploded with the confirmation it wasn't just me who thought so. We didn't belong here. It was clear.

"We need to get out of here before they kill us," I whispered.

He pulled away from my words. "They won't kill you. You just need to prove to them you've been rehabilitated. Then get released."

"You don't understand," I retorted. "They don't plan to release us. They just want to suppress us. Control us. We're doomed here."

His eyebrows pulled in as if confused.

I added, "Can you help us?"

He took two steps up the stairs to create more space between us. "I don't know. I don't want to lose my job." He took another step.

I'd asked too much of him too soon.

"Well, you actually really helped me right now," I said. "Thank you."

He smiled. "Get back to your room before they find you. No telling what will happen if you're caught way over here."

"Okay, I will."

"Okay, then," he said as he took another step. "See you around?"

"Yup. Thanks, Patrick."

His eyes brightened at the sound of his name. I'd never actually said it before to him, but we all knew his name.

"You're welcome..." And he hung on his words.

"Grace," I said.

He smiled again. "You're welcome. Grace."

I flew down the stairs, passing the alluring door to the second floor which tempted me to return to its safety, and instead, I continued to the first floor. Getting to Emma was my primary focus now, but my unexpected encounter with Patrick thrummed through my mind nonstop.

He knew we didn't belong here, and that validation was exactly what I'd needed. And the relief of finding a rational staff member excited every bone in my body. He would help us. I was sure of it.

Sneaking through the dark corridor and passing the grand foyer area, I tiptoed to the alcove that hid the passage to The Hole.

Pulling the heavy door open, I listened for any sign of movement or activity within. Silence wafted up to me and I slipped into the darkness, closing the door behind me.

My bare feet gripped the cold stone stairs, sending a shuddering chill through my body. The dull glow of the lamp lit my way while casting ominous shadows all around. I flinched at every dark corner, certain demons lurked, ready to grab me as I passed.

I moved beyond the room of suitcases, then stood at the door to Emma's prison while my heart pounded in my ears. With a quick breath, I opened it and stepped inside.

Gasping, Emma sat straight up. Her head twitched as she struggled to identify who had just entered her cell.

"Emma," I whispered. "It's me."

"Thank fucking Christ," she shouted. "I'm losing my mind in here, Grace. Get me out!"

When she pulled on her restraints, she grimaced in pain.

"Stop struggling." I hurried over to her, then pushed her shoulder down on the metal slab. "You'll only make it worse." Blood at her wrists and ankles proved she'd been pulling against the straps. "It will be morning soon, and you'll be released."

"What if you're wrong?" she shot back. "What if they leave me here to rot? Having me out of the way is what they want."

I exhaled loudly. She was right.

"Emma." I adjusted the peacoat over her. "It's true. They don't intend to make us well in any way. They only plan to silence us." I paused, remembering her file. "We can't let them."

Her eyes narrowed as she stared at me through the darkness. "What are you talking about?"

"Lobotomy."

Her breath hissed out of her. "How do you know?"

"The files, Emma. I read them."

Her head dropped with a bang. "I knew it," she whispered. "That fucking shrink. The prick put his hand on my knee. His fingers went under the hem of my frock. I should have let him."

"What?" My shrill voice bounced off the damp walls.

"He just wanted to fuck. I should have let him." She turned her head away from me. "When I pushed his hand away..." She hesitated. "I called him a sleazy old man. As soon as I said it, his face turned red, like it would burst. I knew I was screwed."

My voice squeaked out of me. "He did that to you?"

"Oh, Grace. You're so naive," she scoffed, her voice turning sour. "That man made me suck his cock more times than I can count. Every session. It was the only way I kept myself from a fucking lobotomy this long." She huffed. "But fucking is a whole different level. *I* choose who I fuck. And no one can take that from me. Not without a fight."

I twitched as my nerves over-loaded. It was too much for me to process. The abuse in this place was never-ending. It had no restrictions.

Her strong will continued to prevail though. She'd been victimized, but still had the ability to hold onto who she was, to her convictions, in such a house of horrors.

"You did the right thing," I said. "Screw that asshole. The Hole is better than allowing him to take you."

"Exactly." She eyed me. "Fuck 'em." She shifted under the coat, unable to resist her natural instinct to escape. "What are we going to do now?"

"I'll stay here as long as possible, but then I'll need to take the coat."

She nodded, and I went on.

"You'll be cold, maybe for just a couple of hours." I shook my head in disgust. "They'll be suspicious why the door is unlocked, so just act like it was their fault."

My head jerked in response to the sound of footsteps from above, I froze. My eyes moved around the darkness of the room as I strained to listen.

"You better get out of here," Emma whispered. "I'll be fine. I have my ways of staying warm." She shook her chaffed wrists and ankles as evidence.

"Okay." I swallowed hard. "I know it will be near impossible, but be as sweet and compliant as possible when they come for you," I said. "Maybe even apologize."

"Hell no," she shouted. "No apologies. But I'll do anything else to be sure I get to see Bobby again."

Chuckling quietly at her defiance, I reveled in the fact they hadn't broken her. Yet.

I reluctantly pulled the peacoat off her, moving toward the door.

"Okay, I'll see you for breakfast." I prayed my words would make it true.

"Get out of here," she demanded, but not before I caught the glimmer of a tear in her eye.

I clicked the door closed behind me, then scurried to the other room to return the coat. Adrenaline pumped through my veins as I threw it into its case before flying up the stone stairs.

My mind spiraled from the story of the abuse from the psychiatrist. His corruption held the power to ruin lives. There was truly no one we could trust here. Except maybe Patrick. But, truly, we were on our own. We just needed to stay one step ahead, at all times, to survive.

I pushed the door open, then peered down the dark corridor by the foyer. My ears perked up as I listened for any sign of movement. Then I snuck out, closing the door behind me. The handle clacked into place with a mind-shattering sound that seemed to resonate throughout the entire ward, and I froze. Waiting for my inevitable execution.

In the dark silence of the hallway, I breathed again and raced toward the stairwell that would lead me back to my room. When I turned the corner, I stopped short. A gasp escaped my throat as I prepared for the impact of a person running straight for me.

My eyes closed as I braced myself. In an instant, the frenzied runner collided into me, and I grabbed on to her shoulders to keep her from taking us both down. I fell against the wall, keeping my grip on her struggling body.

"Let me go," she squealed. "I need to get home."

I pushed her from my hold to see her face. It was the new girl who I'd seen registering earlier in the evening.

"You can't leave now," I whispered through my crazed condition. "The doors are all locked."

I glanced toward the foyer, recognizing how easy it was for her to come in. But leaving was a whole different story. It was impossible. Once the ward had hold of you, it never let go.

"I don't belong here." She struggled out of my hold. "Help me. Where are my belongings? They took them from me."

It wouldn't be long before her suitcase found its way into The Hole with the rest of ours. Our identities. Our lives.

I caught the slightest haze of dawn's light breaking through the windows of the foyer.

"The morning staff will come around any time now," I said. "If you get caught..."

Her eyes held mine without blinking. "I don't care if I get caught. I don't belong here," she snapped. "The man in the Administration Building, Dr. Johnson. He's wrong. He doesn't understand."

"Please, you don't know how they are here." I moved a few steps toward the stairwell. "If we get caught out of our rooms, we'll be in a lot of trouble."

I reached for her, waving my other fingers to get her to follow me. But then my mind fixated on one thing only—the name she had just mentioned. Dr. Johnson. It sounded so familiar, and I struggled to picture his face.

"Come on," I said. "Back to your room. We can talk about your plan of leaving at breakfast."

Thomas. The name flashed in my mind. *Dr. Thomas Johnson.* He was the one who did my intake here. His eyes had held concern, like he saw *me.* He didn't just see a loon who'd been sanctioned by her unwell mother. He saw...*me.*

The new girl stood rigid like a statue as tears fell from her eyes.

"You have to come," I repeated. "Now!"

Her head shook. "He told my parents it was hysteria. He said time at the asylum could make me well again."

"They say that about all of us," I whispered, inching closer to the stairs. Panic rose in me as I worried about the morning staff.

"But I don't need to be here. I need my dolls. And my cups." Her voice cracked. "I want my rocks and my pieces of wallpaper. They need to be arranged just so. If anyone touches them…"

I fought to hide my surprise at her words. She actually sounded delirious, and I considered running from her for my own safety. Maybe she *did* belong here.

I turned to the stairs. One last time, I waved my hand for her to follow me. If she didn't come, I'd leave without her. After a moment, she stepped forward and joined me.

"Hurry. This way." I scurried around the corner into the stairwell. With a smashing blow, I barreled into a white blur of fabric.

I pushed to get around the solid barrier, but it moved with me, blocking my way.

"And what is this?" Her evil tone etched claw marks into my brain. "Runaways?"

My eyes lifted in horror to meet the glare of my nemesis. Nurse Totten.

She straightened her cap and growled again. "You know the punishment for being out…"

My voice shot out of me before I could control it. "She was lost. I heard her crying, so I came to help her."

Nurse Totten's glare shot to the new girl, who cowered at my back.

"Miss Kate." Totten tipped her head to see her. "Are you lost, Kate?"

She hid behind me, voice a murmur.

"Speak up," Totten commanded.

"Yes," Kate squeaked.

Nurse Totten leaned closer. "You're not to be out of your room, or off your floor at night. The rules are rigid. I thought I made that clear to you."

She narrowed her eyes, studying me as she spoke to Kate.

"Yes, ma'am," Kate whispered. "I got confused in the darkness."

Totten's eyes pierced into my soul, searching for my intentions. "Take her back to her room," she barked at me. Her sideways glare shot my nerves as if she was seeing right through me. But something else seemed to hold her attention as well. She was up to something.

"Yes, ma'am," I said, repeating Kate's respectful words.

I grabbed Kate's hand, hurriedly I pulled her up the stairs. She stumbled along like her legs were too weak to carry her. Turning back to see if Totten was following us, I watched her shadow move along the first-floor corridor in the direction of the alcove.

My heart stopped, halting my feet as well.

Totten was heading toward Emma's dungeon.

CHAPTER 8

With no sign of Emma's release, my breakfast stuck in my throat. If Nurse Totten had decided to leave her down there in The Hole any longer, I'd lose my mind. She didn't deserve it. No one did.

The punishments around here never seemed to fit the crime, and I promised myself I'd report it at the first opportunity. I'd tell someone who cared. Maybe the superintendent, Dr. Thomas Johnson. His kind eyes and gentle mannerisms were the only sign of humanity around here, except for Patrick's. But Dr. Johnson held a position of great authority that might actually have the power to make changes.

I stirred my clumped porridge as I spoke to Kaitlin.

"I'm worried," I said.

"Yeah, me too," she agreed. "It's been too long. Too much time in the cold. Alone." She glanced out the window.

A rhythmic pounding entered the dining hall, and my ears perked up. *Bang. Bang. Bang.*

I twitched in my seat. "Bobby's outside," I whisper-screamed. "Maybe he knows what happened the other night."

Kaitlin pulled back. "I'm not getting caught talking to him." Her head shook. "No way. And plus, isn't he a killer?"

"Don't be a wimp." I poked her rib. "We just can't be seen. That's all." I glanced toward the staff table and noted their intense focus on their eggs and potatoes. "We have fresh-air time after breakfast, so we'll just be hanging around the green anyway.

"I didn't hear Rotten call us for yard time." Kaitlin's eyes narrowed.

"It wasn't Rotten. The dining staff said it when we first arrived," I reminded her. "They told us to bring the trash to the dumpsters before fresh air, so…"

Kaitlin glanced at the staff table, watching as Nurse Totten cut a thick piece of ham and speared it with her fork.

The basketball continued to pound outside, calling for us to come out to it.

As soon as one of the day nurses announced the end of the meal, I hopped up and brought my bowl to the counter. I reached my hand out, asking for a trash barrel. One of the workers pushed a can out from behind the partition. Once I grabbed it, I pulled it toward the door, motioning for Kaitlin to follow my lead.

I banged the barrel down the steps of the dining hall, then dragged it across the pavement toward the dumpster. My head turned in the direction of the bouncing sound, and I met Bobby's waiting eyes.

And standing beside him, separated by metal fencing, was Emma!

Every nerve in my body jolted to life as Emma grinned. I dropped my grip from the barrel, then charged toward her.

"Emma," I squealed. "When did you get out?"

She twisted her finger in the space between the chain-link fencing near Bobby. "Nothing to worry about, Grace. They can never hold me for long."

Bobby smirked, eyes on her fingers gripping the fencing.

"Too hot to handle," he murmured.

She rolled her eyes. "Oh, Grace, this is Bobby. He's here for murdering his parents." She leaned her hip against the fence.

"Pleased to meet you," I said with a nod. My eyes dropped to the ground as I silently roasted myself for not having a cooler reply, like Emma. But she'd also caught me off guard with her casual reference to his heinous crime—or the accusation, anyway. Even if he did have no memory of it, it was still serious.

"What landed *you* in here?" he asked.

My spine straightened. Wasn't that information private? Why did he think he could just ask such a thing? Maybe Emma had set the bar, blurting out his infraction against society. I supposed I owed him a reply then.

"Oh, I, um…" I stuttered. "I was thrown from a horse and ah…"

"Incarcerated for being an equestrian?" he teased.

My face grew hot. "No, I hurt my head. A brain injury, I guess. They said I had brain fever." I shrugged my shoulders.

"Are you serious?" he shouted. "Those assholes."

"I know," Emma interjected. "They create whatever they want in the charts to make us look nuts. What else did you find in the records?"

I eye-balled her to shut up. I had no idea who Bobby was and if he could be trusted.

"It's okay. I already told him," she teased.

I glanced back to be sure no one was watching us. "It's all made up shit. Head injuries, melancholia, disappointment. I'm honestly beginning to believe none of us actually belong in here."

Bobby stepped closer to the fence, then pressed his forehead into it.

"Hey, thanks," he said. "You'd be the first."

His words caught me by surprise. It almost sounded like he wanted his story to finally be heard. To be believed. But no one around here would listen. They just trap you and throw away the key.

My head tipped as I studied him. "What happened the other night when you guys were caught together?"

Emma giggled and tried to squeeze her fingers further through the fencing. Bobby touched the tips.

"My security guard," he said. "Sometimes I can slip out of his smothering grasp. You know, he has a secret little problem with the drink." He tipped his hand at his mouth to mimic sipping alcohol. He looked to the other side of the court and nodded to the guard. "But he doesn't like when I take advantage of that. He gets a little...mean." He rubbed his head and I suddenly noticed the swollen bruise at his temple.

"And Rotten wasted no time when I was delivered back to the ward," Emma added. "It was like the bitch had The Hole ready for me, looking forward to the torture."

Bobby let out a loud exhale, as if recalling the details of their separation. "The true torture was being pulled apart. We'll be more careful next time."

Emma purred in agreement and blew at his face.

I half-swiveled behind me to avoid their intimate interaction but also to find Kaitlin. She stood at the dumpster, holding her trash can, mid-dump, and stared at us with her jaw unhinged. Her expression cracked me up, and I laughed.

Emma and Bobby eyed her and laughed, too.

"She's the prude," Emma said with a chuckle.

I blasted the evil eye at Emma, then waved Kaitlin over. She lowered her can before taking small, slow steps toward us.

"And so what does that make me?" I stared at Emma.

"The smart one," she stated.

Instead of deflecting an expected insult, I took her words and allowed them to soak in. I liked to think I was smart, but this place was powerful enough to create doubts. But Emma was right. I was going to think our way out of here. Outsmart them all.

Turning to Bobby, I asked, "Why do they let you play basketball all the time? No offense, but I'd think they'd keep you in high security. Especially after the other night."

He shrugged. "Beats me. Must be some elite-privilege thing. You know, entitlement." He rolled the basketball between his hands. "I guess they feel bad taking a college athlete off the court. They figure, hey, if this guy was in college, he's probably not *that* bad."

"Seriously?" I argued. "That's so unfair!"

"Whoa, easy with your judgment," he shot back, reaching for his heart in feigned offense. "It's not my fault they're sports fans." He chuckled.

"It's because they're uncertain," Emma interjected.

"About what?" I asked.

"You know, he doesn't remember any of it." She raised an eyebrow at Bobby. "So who knows what really happened."

"It's tough to punish someone to the full extent," Bobby added, "when there's a shadow of a doubt." A sinister grin crossed his face.

My eyes darted to Emma's to see if she got the same creepy vibe from him, but she was too busy batting her lashes to notice.

"Emma, you're out," Kaitlin gushed as she reached us.

"Yup. Time to party." She gestured to Bobby. "Kaitlin, meet Bobby."

Kaitlin remained a good distance from the fence, sheltering herself behind me. "Hi," she replied with a slight flick of her hand.

He shrugged off her avoidance. "So, a couple of my buddies from Springfield College are coming up to visit on Saturday," he said. "You girls should meet them. Good guys."

"Oh, we can't," Kaitlin replied first. "We're not allowed."

I elbowed her ribs. "What she means to say is that it's not easy to get away from, you know, the wardens." I looked at the dining hall door, sure the staff watched us in that very moment, but there wasn't any sign of them yet.

Emma cleared her throat, stepping directly in front of him. "What they mean to say is—what day and what time?"

As soon as Nurse Totten emerged from the dining hall, we scattered away from the court. Bobby had just started telling us about secret underground tunnels at the asylum but then quickly moved to the far side, out of sight. He shot his ball at the basket as if nothing else in the world mattered.

"Wait," Kaitlin whispered as we hurried to the green by the chapel. "Do you think he meant what he said about the underground tunnels?"

"Of course he did," Emma replied. "I trust him."

"Well, we can't believe everything he tells us," I said. "We don't even know him. And well, you know, he's here for a reason."

"So cautious," Emma interjected. "Worrywart." Then she slowed and gathered us around her. "I've heard of the underground tunnels before. They're legendary. The older patients speak of them, but no one's ever seen them."

Kaitlin shook her head.

"Don't have a full-on panic attack, Kaitlin." Emma adjusted Kaitlin's frock. "We'll find the tunnels. At night. So no worries."

Kaitlin's eyes nearly fell out of her head.

I couldn't blame her for panicking. The idea of hidden underground tunnels, with a murderer and his friends, scared the shit out of me, too. But, honestly, it was our only opportunity at experiencing some real life. Freedom.

"We'll do it," I stated as I locked elbows with Kaitlin. "We deserve to, Kaitlin. We don't deserve seclusion, punishment, and locked doors. We're young women who need to live. Let's do this!"

Her shoulders sank, but she tightened elbows with me at the same time.

"Do you really think there's a billiards table down there?" Kaitlin whispered, remembering Bobby's descriptions of mysterious secret rooms in the tunnels.

"Hah!" Emma exclaimed. "'Atta girl!" She smacked Kaitlin on the back. "Now, what day did Bobby say his friends were coming?"

CHAPTER 9

Five days and counting to find the hidden tunnels before Bobby's friends arrived. For the first time since I could remember, the days of the week suddenly mattered and helped me measure time.

I flipped the fabric of an old gray frock to line up the hem, then turned the crank of my Singer to get the needle moving again. Eyes on Kaitlin, I giggled as she fumbled with her machine, which entangled a web of thread over her garment. She pulled at it, making the snarled mess even worse.

Emma sat at her machine, picking at her nails, while the girls around her worked like slaves.

"Mending-time is bull crap," she whispered. "I don't sew."

"At least fake it," I said through pinched lips. "So you don't lose privileges. We need to stay squeaky clean."

"Yeah. Yeah." She leaned back. "Even the music room is better than this."

A nursemaid by the door caught a glimpse of Emma's defiance, then scurried over to the head nurse. Within seconds, the head nurse bombed toward Emma with a stealthy glare in her eye.

"Back to work," she demanded, with a clip at the back of Emma's head. "You're not to waste your time here."

Emma sat up as if shocked by the accusation and the assault.

"Oh, my misunderstanding," she said. "I was under the impression this was a therapeutic training activity for us. You know, to assist with our rehabilitation." Every single syllable dripped with sarcasm.

"Are you refusing to engage?" the nurse shot back.

Jeannie whimpered from behind Emma. Any hint of conflict sent her scurrying for her teddy bear.

"I don't think it fits my recovery recommendations," Emma continued. "I need something more...civilized."

The nurse's face turned beet red.

"I'd say you wouldn't recognize civilized if it was dropped in front of your face. Now get sewing or I'll report your saucy defiance to Nurse Totten."

"Defiance?" Emma said. "*Now* this is defiance? A punishable offense? Sewing therapy? More like labor camp." She paused as if attempting to hold back her next words, but she failed. "One small step behind being a nurse in a madhouse."

"Up!" The nurse reached for Emma's arm, then pulled.

Emma resisted her tug, clinging to her chair.

"No, no, no," Jeannie squealed, rocking in her seat.

"You'll come with me at once," the nurse repeated.

Jeannie's wails grew louder as her rocking nearly knocked her off her chair.

Betty stood from her seat, a row away, and called over, "Nurse Riley, Emma wasn't feeling well on our way here." She glanced at Emma with lifted brows, as if to get her to play along. "She was too embarrassed to say anything. You know, girl troubles. She said it was causing a migraine."

Emma reached for her head, swaying like she was woozy.

"It's no excuse for belligerence and insults." The nurse scanned the room, noticing all sewing had ceased. Every girl refused to continue her work until the situation was resolved. And their judging stares made clear how the resolution should play out. "I'll report you if you cause another moment's trouble." She dropped Emma's arm after one final squeeze, then returned to guard the door. "Now, sew," she called, voice booming through the room.

Jeannie's hands pressed over her ears as she crouched on the floor under her machine. "They'll take you to the burrow," she whispered. "You'll lose yourself there. Like the gophers." Her fingers tapped along her head like scurrying feet.

I leaned in closer to hear Jeannie's small voice better. "What gophers?"

"Creeping. Creeping. Through the darkness." Jeannie's fingers played through the air, moving in various directions.

I glanced at Emma. Her shrug seemed to say, "Lost cause," as she reached for a frock from her pile.

Kaitlin cracked her knuckles, then cranked the wheel of her Singer. Her flinching shoulders proved her attempt to disguise her panic attack. Smiling to myself, I caught Betty's worried eyes. "Thank you," I mouthed silently, knowing she had just saved Emma's hide from another stint in The Hole.

The hum of the sewing machines helped calm the tension in the room, but my mind continued to fester on Jeannie's words. She knew of a place we were unfamiliar with. The burrow, she'd called it. I couldn't help but wonder who'd taken her there and why.

Running a ripped hem through my machine, I kept watch of Emma from the corner of my eye. She pushed a wad of gray fabric under the needle, holding the wheel at the side. Her gaze went beyond the sewing machine, out into oblivion, as her hand hung on to the wheel with a grasp that turned her knuckles white.

"Emma?" I whispered.

She blinked, then squinted over at me. Her empty eyes held mine for a moment, then blurred out as if seeing nothing.

"Emma? Are you okay?" I asked.

Her eyes focused on me like she was just returning from a dream.

"Grace. I need to get out of here," she mouthed. "They're going to kill me."

I knew she was referring to the threat of lobotomy and I shook my head at her.

With one more breath she added, "But I refuse to give them the satisfaction."

～

Several needle puncture wounds later—after spending the majority of the day sewing—we were allowed to hang out in the common room. I actually enjoyed the room with the old couches, the half-broken radio, and windows that actually allowed some sunlight in. It was the closest thing to a family living room in the ward, and it offered a sick feeling of home in my gut.

Kaitlin and I claimed the couch by the big window immediately, while Emma walked through the room checking in with the other girls. We had a thousand puzzle pieces spread across the coffee table in front of us, two sides of the edges finished.

"I feel nauseous." I rubbed my middle, knowing it had nothing to do with my stomach. "It's like a sinister feeling growing within me. We need to get out of here, Kaitlin."

"I know." She nodded.

"No, I'm serious. I'm not just talking in general. I mean, if we want to live, if we want to have a life, we need to get out of here before they make it so we can't."

Kaitlin dropped the puzzle piece she was fiddling with. "We just have to bide our time. Stay out of trouble."

"No. It's not that simple. They won't allow it." I glanced around the room for any nosy staff members, but a woman pacing and moaning at the far side of the room distracted them. "They don't care about us getting well. They only care about keeping everyone under control and subdued."

"So why can't we just lay low?" she asked.

"It's not enough. And for how long?" I fidgeted with the puzzle to make it look like we were busy. "It's impossible to follow their rules without losing ourselves, Kaitlin. We'll turn into mindless minions. And if we don't, they'll do it for us."

"What are you talking about?"

Emma trotted over, then stopped by the window. Jeannie crouched on the floor under the pane with her knees pulled into her chest. She continued to rock. Emma stood over her, kicking out at her feet. Jeannie was unresponsive except for a slight whimper. Emma shrugged before moving over to us. She plopped down on the coffee table, right on top of the puzzle pieces.

"Bonjour, ladies," she sang. "A fine afternoon we have. Don't you agree?" She flipped her hair, arching her back.

Kaitlin leaned into Emma, then whispered, "Grace thinks they're going to hurt us, like, actually hurt us."

Emma stifled a laugh. "Are you serious? Of course they are." She eyed me as if to confirm Kaitlin was for real. "Sweetie, we're not getting out of here alive. It's in our files. Just ask Grace. She's got all the goods on us."

Kaitlin's face twisted in fear. "But that would be murder. The place would be shut down."

"Oh, no. They wouldn't be that stupid," Emma added. "They just turn us into zombies. Brain dead. Much easier to manage—a lot quieter. But to the outside world, not dead."

The moaning woman at the far side of the room grew more agitated as the staff tried to calm her. Something had set her off, and she started banging her head on the wall. A nursemaid tried to stop her, but the woman outweighed her.

"Get an orderly," the nursemaid called. "And Nurse Totten."

I sucked in a deep breath. The last thing we needed was Nurse Totten anywhere near us, especially here in the common room. She was the most dangerous and unpredictable variable in the ward.

Within minutes, Patrick flew into the lounge. His white outfit made him stand out among the gray. I watched as he approached the hysterical woman, expecting him drag her out. Instead, he stood by her and spoke gently.

"Tilly. Tilly. Look at me," he said. "Come on, Tilly. Just look at me. You're going to be okay."

Tilly stomped like a child, continuing to bang her head against the wall.

Smiling into her eyes, he soothed her as he slipped a pillow between her and the wall. "Tilly, relax. They'll take you for a warm bath. You can sing as much as you like, and you'll feel better."

She slowed her swaying, meeting his eyes.

"It's okay to feel scared sometimes," he continued. "But then, you can take care of yourself and start to feel better…"

Rotten stormed into the room, cutting him off. The shock of her presence shattered the calm Patrick had provided.

"Hold her," Nurse Totten commanded him.

Patrick's eyes widened as he caught a glimpse of the huge needle in her hand. The glass vile held a clear liquid.

"She's calm now," he stated quickly.

But it was too late.

Totten jabbed the needle into Tilly's arm, causing the poor woman to flail from the shock of the assault. She threw her arms wide, knocking Nurse Totten away. Within seconds, though, the sedative drooped her eyes and slumped her shoulders. When she wobbled, Patrick caught her, practically having to drag her dead weight to the armchair in the corner. Before she hit the cushion, she was out.

Nurse Totten straightened her square cap, then fussily rubbed the creases out of her uniform. "We need to keep the peace here," she called to everyone in the room. All eyes were on her. "Don't be the next to cause a disturbance. We won't have it around here." As she clomped her heels across the wood floor, she snapped, "Patrick, get back to the station to finish your work."

Before Patrick retreated from Tilly, he checked one last time to be sure she was breathing and comfortable. He glanced around the room, stalling on me. A small smile lifted the edges of his mouth before he moved to follow Totten.

"Someone has a crush on Gracey," Emma sang.

"Shut up!" I rolled my eyes. "That's not true. He just…helped me."

I continued to stare at the door he'd left through, still hearing his kind, calming words to Tilly. Why couldn't the rest of the staff work with the patients that way? It was all they needed. A little compassion. Redirection. Kindness. Was it that hard?

"He helped you?" Emma flicked a puzzle piece at me. "Do tell."

Shaking my head, I threw it back at her.

"When I snuck into the office last night, I bumped into him after." I remembered every detail of the encounter. My senses had been on high alert, picking up on every vibration before I smashed into him. "He didn't report me. He just let me...go."

Kaitlin glanced around the room for any eavesdroppers. "Can you tell us about our files now? I don't think I can wait any longer. Just tell us the important stuff."

Appearing bored, Emma stuck out her tongue. "I know exactly what mine says. I can see it all over the doc's face, everything he thinks of me. He's a pig."

"Tell me, Grace. Please," Kaitlin pressed.

Kaitlin's jaw hung open as I told her about her file—head trauma, congestion of the brain, quackery. Emma burst out laughing.

"Jesus! A bump on the head and you're sent to an asylum?" Emma scoffed. "At least I left a trail of destruction behind *me*. Broken hearts, mostly. But baffled authority figures as well. Victims of my superiority, you could say."

We paused, waiting for her to say she was just kidding or exaggerating. But she didn't flinch.

Kaitlin rubbed the side of her head. "I don't remember how I hit it."

Her obvious confusion about how she ended up here was sad. None of us really understood how our fates landed us in a place like this. Even with the information from the files, we were left with uncertainty and questions. All we knew for sure was that it was wrong.

"Apparently, I was thrown from a horse." I rubbed my head in the same way Kaitlin had. "But I'm fuzzy on the details, too."

"It's annoying that they say I have a nervous nature," Kaitlin mumbled.

Emma laughed again. Harder.

Sarcastically, Kaitlin added, "And what the hell is suppression of menses? My God! They need to mind their own business!"

"It just means you have an irregular period," Emma said. "Men just can't handle anything to do with that topic, so they turn it into insanity." She hesitated. "Or they go to the extreme, twisting our sexuality, and call it nymphomania. They still pull women off the streets in California and 'examine them' for diseases if they look even suspiciously sexual."

Emma's shoulders squared as if she were proud of her nympho label.

"Fuck 'em," she added.

"Either way, our files are bullshit," I said. "There's nothing wrong with us. Even Patrick said so. But on paper, we're loons."

Emma interrupted. "So basically, we're fucked."

We fiddled with the puzzle pieces to keep attention off our conversation. Emma turned a piece over and over in her fingers.

"So Patrick thinks we're normal? she asked out of nowhere.

I smiled with a nod.

She added, "So, what are we going to do, Genius?"

I thought about our options. None of us had family who would save us. It was clear they'd abandoned us here, for shame or out of necessity. It didn't matter. What mattered was we were on our own and it was up to us to correct our situation.

"We need to find someone on the outside who can help us," I mused. "We would need a place to stay. And then get jobs."

"Like what—secretaries?" Emma asked. "No thanks! That's no different from being a prisoner here. I'm thinking more like parties, music halls, cocktails, jazz, and dancing the foxtrot."

I smirked at her grandiose plans.

"No, something like starting our own business," I said. "We know how to sew now. We can open a shop for tailoring, then create our own designs. Like, bringing women's fashion forward, with comfort and function." My mind swam with dreams of becoming something great.

For once, Emma didn't have a snide remark. Instead, she seemed to think about what I'd suggested.

"Bobby can help us," she said. "He has lots of connections on the outside." She stared out the window as if planning our next moves.

"We need to find the tunnels," I whispered. "They are the one way we can plan in private."

"Exactly what I was just thinking," Emma agreed. "And Bobby thinks he can find a way into them, too. His night guard is passed out half the time, and well, I think he believes Bobby's innocent anyway."

Kaitlin continued rubbing her head, as if the plan was too much to follow. "How do you trust Bobby so much when you only just met him? You actually know nothing about him." She pushed back into the couch cushions.

"Actually, Missy, I know more about him than I even know about you." Emma's tone stung causing Kaitlin to wince. "You don't share a single truth about yourself. Ever. I have to figure you out through observation. It gets tedious."

"I'm just saying…" Kaitlin attempted to recover. "He's in here for a violent crime. I just want you to stay safe."

"I can take care of myself, thank you," Emma retorted. "Bobby and I have a connection. It was instant. I know his soul. And he knows mine. And the fact that we met here, it's bizarre, but it's also beautiful."

She stared at Kaitlin until she looked away.

The tension in their exchange didn't ruffle me in the slightest though. Emma was free to do what she wanted, crazy as it all seemed. But love was funny like that. It didn't always make sense.

Instead, my focus remained on planning our next steps to get out of here.

"I bet Patrick could help us," I murmured. "He knows every inch of this place."

"Bingo!" Emma pointed her finger at me. "It's up to you now, Grace."

I dropped my head back. It would be difficult finding time to conspire with Patrick. And he'd be protective of his job, knowing to not get caught cavorting with the patients.

"I can try," I agreed.

But then Emma stated, "No, you can *do*."

CHAPTER 10

My eyes refused to close as I lay in my bed plotting a way to find the secret underground tunnels connecting the wards. When I had gone to find Emma in The Hole, I had no memory of any other doors beside hers and the suitcase room. Access to the tunnels had to be somewhere else. I considered the size of the ward, realizing there had to be another section to the basement besides the stone cellar where they'd restrained us. Maybe hidden in plain sight.

My feet twitched and I shifted positions, wishing I had my pillow back. It just wasn't worth upsetting Jeannie, though. In order to keep the peace, the teddy bear needed it more than me.

Wails echoed from down the hall, then clomping heels passed our room. When the wails turned to screams, I covered my ears, wishing it away. Whoever it was, they'd end up like Tilly, drugged and strapped to their bed for days. My lips pressed into a white line as my hands balled into fists.

"Once I was crazy 'bout a man." Jeannie's voice tickled at the back of my mind. "Mine all mine." She sang quietly in her bed. "Trouble, trouble. It seems that troubles going to follow me to my grave."

I rolled to face her as she sang to me. Her voice was soft as an angel's, and she repeated a final line like a skipping record.

"Downhearted blues," she crooned. "Downhearted blues." Her voice was barely audible. "Downhearted blues," she mouthed.

I shifted away from her.

"Downhearted blues," she repeated.

I peeked at her again before facing the wall as the wails in the hall grew louder. I was truly in a nuthouse and was sure I was losing my own mind, a little bit each day. As I glanced at her again, I jerked to avoid her face hitting mine.

Jeannie was out of her bed, hovering over mine as she sung into my ear. I pulled my blanket up to my chin, staring into her harrowing eyes.

"You'll lose yourself in the burrows," she whispered. "A labyrinth of darkness. It takes your soul away."

My eyes shot wide. "What are you talking about? Get back in bed."

"The burrows," she said. "You mustn't go."

Her words sent fear coursing through my veins, my heart pounding wildly. She was crazy. I waved my hand to get her to return to her bed. But was she?

"Go back to bed before you're caught," I whispered.

Acting scolded, her face pinched in sadness and bottom lip pushed out as her shoulders drooped. Her lip trembled, and I knew exactly what came next.

"Jeannie, it's okay. I'm not mad." I smiled for extra affect. "Thank you for telling me. You're a good friend." I prayed my praise would stop her tantrum before it started.

"Do I still have to go to my room?" she asked.

Holy shit. She was nuts. It was like she'd regressed to her former life, and thought I was her parent. Playing along was the only way to get her away from me.

"No, Jeannie. Of course not," I said. "You're a good girl. Thank you for warning me about that…place. I'll give you candies in the morning for being so good."

An enormous smile crossed her face as she squeezed her bear, then bounced on her heels. "Please, please, please," she sang.

"Tuck Bear in now, nice and cozy, so he will be ready for the sweets, too." Again, I motioned toward her bed.

"Yes," she said, turning to her pillows. "I will. Thank you."

After inhaling, I let it out slowly as relief moved through me.

Jeannie arranged her pillows in twenty different ways before finding the perfect spot for her bear. She sang under her breath as she worked. "Downhearted blues…downhearted blues…" And the gentle words lulled me toward sleep.

Then my eyes sprang open again.

The burrows!

A labyrinth where people could get lost.

Jeannie must have been listening to us in the common room. Tucked in a ball under the window, she had appeared comatose.

But she'd been listening.

And she knew of the secret tunnels we were searching for.

She'd been in them.

～

We lined up, single file, and marched to the dining hall for breakfast. It was my first opportunity to talk to Kaitlin and Emma, and I felt as if I would burst out of my skin.

"I think Jeannie knows how to get to the tunnels," I whispered.

They flanked me on both sides, pressing for details.

I continued. "I think she's been in them."

Emma scanned the line for Jeannie.

I hit her arm. "No, she's sensitive. The tunnels scare her. She calls them the burrows. Said they'll take your soul. Weird shit like that." I searched the line for her as well. "I'll handle Jeannie."

"You need to get her to show you where they are," Emma pressed.

"Maybe during laundry?" I murmured.

"What if you get caught?" Kaitlin whispered. "Jeannie's a mess. She'll make it so obvious."

"I'll find a way to trick her," I said. "She's like a little kid. If I make it seem like a game, it just might work."

Apprehensive, Kaitlin shook her head. "I don't know. We just can't afford to get on Rotten's bad side again."

Just as she spoke the words, Nurse Totten came into view. She stood at the side of the line, inspecting each girl as we passed. Eluding notice, Kaitlin and Emma moved into single file again, and we passed with our eyes glued to the ground in submission. The glare of her steely eyes bored into my back, and I was sure she could see right through me.

As we finished our porridge and prepared to return to the ward for laundry duty, a familiar pounding resonated through the walls from outside.

Emma's eyes lit up, and she grabbed my arm. "It's Bobby!"

She hurried to clear her dishes, gesturing for us to follow her. I glanced toward the staff table, but they remained focused on their buttered toast and bacon.

"Keep watch by the door," she said. "If they get up, cause a distraction until I get back."

Before I could refuse, she was out the door.

Terrified, I stared into Kaitlin's face. What if they noticed Emma missing? She took too many risks. She was literally insane. My heart pounded in my ears as I struggled to appear normal. The more I tried to remain calm, the more my muscles twitched and my eyes darted about.

Kaitlin was even worse. She began pacing, nervously running her hands through her hair. Her breathing became erratic, and I knew one of her panic attacks was looming just around the corner.

"Kaitlin, breathe," I whispered as I glanced toward the staff table.

Certain they must all be staring at us, I flickered my eyes toward them, every screaming nerve in my body telling me not to. Just as my eyes reached their table, my shoulder jolted, causing me to stumble forward.

Emma had smashed into us, out of breath and giggling.

"Did they notice?" She eyed the staff table.

"Shit! Don't do that," I barked. "You gave me a heart attack!"

She laughed. "Sissies." Twisting a lock of her hair in her fingers, she singsonged, "I told him we'd find the tunnels tonight."

Kaitlin gasped. "Jesus, Emma."

"What?" She reeled back in feigned offense. "I didn't do anything. Grace is the one who figured out a way." She pointed at me.

I snuck a peek over at Jeannie. She went about her breakfast routine, talking to herself and blinking with childlike innocence. It would be easy to trick her, and I wasn't sure if I should feel guilty or grateful about it.

As we filed out of the dining hall, I shifted my position to be next to her in line. Gaining her trust throughout the day was my new mission.

"When do I get my sweets?" She clipped my heels as she crept up close behind me.

"Oh." I smiled. "Soon. I promise."

"Oh, goodie." She giggled and bounced with her fingers tapping together.

I walked with her in line, skipping and giggling quietly to keep her entertained. Before long, we were all in the Excited Ward positioned around enormous vats full of sudsy cold water. Mounds of sloppy gray frocks rolled in the tubs as we pushed them around with long wooden poles.

The laundry area was on the lowest floor of the ward and I wondered if access to the tunnels was anywhere near us. I'd never considered it before because this part of the basement was so different from where The Hole was. It was similar to the other floors with white walls and doors with windows in them. It just didn't seem subterranean enough to have access to underground tunnels.

I lifted my eyes to Kaitlin and Emma. They both nudged me closer to Jeannie. Their nervous energy shot over to me like lightning bolts.

When I glanced around the room to locate the staff overseeing our work, I couldn't find Rotten, but the other nursemaids scowled just as she did—probably part of their training program.

A twitch of anxiety ran up my spine, causing me to stand taller. Taking my pole, I shuffled my feet closer to Jeannie.

Plunging my stick into her vat, I pushed at the fabric she worked on, making it easier for her to maneuver. She smiled at me, and I grinned back. We worked her area of the vat until all the frocks had equal agitation, then pulled them out, one by one, for the wringer.

As I placed each frock on the machine, Jeannie cranked the handle. Together, we moved through the work at a steady pace.

"You're good at using the wringer," I praised.

Her eyes lit up. "Thank you." She grinned. "Do I get my sweets now?"

"Oh, yes," I said. "Definitely. But you'll have to come with me to get them."

"Okeydokey," she agreed. "Now?"

I caught the eye of a nursemaid. "Washroom?" I asked her.

The nursemaid nodded approval for me to take a bathroom break.

"Come with me," I said to Jeannie.

She followed me out of the laundry room and into the hall. I looked in both directions, but I saw no clues to where access to the tunnels might be.

Putting my hand on my chin, I rubbed it. "I just can't remember which way," I said.

"To where?"

"To the burrows," I added.

She froze in place, her head frantically shaking. "No..." she whined.

"Don't worry, Jeannie. You don't have to go in," I assured her. "I just need to step inside to find where I hid the sweets." I smiled big.

Her eyes darted down the hall as she considered my words. In that instant, I knew the direction we'd be going.

"Come on," I said with a playful tone, skipping forward a few paces. "It will only take a second."

She shuffled along as her eyes nervously darted about. But soon, she took my lead and started skipping.

I moved faster with more jubilation, and she fully joined in. Slowing a tiny bit, I allowed her to pass me and lead the way. I skipped along right behind her with a light giggle to keep her calm.

We passed several doors, and I glanced into a room with a slightly ajar door. File cabinets lined the walls with brown boxes stacked on the tops. There was a door at the far side leading up to the outside courtyard. Windows at the top of the back wall allowed me to see treetops and blue sky. The room seemed familiar, but I was sure I'd never actually been in it.

At the end of the hall, Jeannie stopped short and her face sagged. Her eyes shot toward a heavy metal door, then back to me.

That was it!

My heart pounded in my ears as excitement filled me. I grabbed onto Jeannie's hand, pulling her along with me back toward the laundry.

"Wait." She resisted. "What about my sweets?"

"We can't get caught, Jeannie. Imagine what Nurse Totten would say. We wouldn't want her to be upset with you, right?"

Her head nodded in rapid bounces.

I continued, "So I'll sneak in there later to get your sweets. I'll surprise you. Okay?"

She glanced toward the metal door, relief relaxing her face. "Okay." But then her face fell. "Just don't go far in there. Or you'll...you'll never come out the same."

Our rendezvous point was so cliché—the washroom. Just like in secondary school. We giggled like giddy children as we gathered by the toilets.

"My heart is pounding." Kaitlin pressed her hand on her chest.

"Mine too," I agreed. "And this was the easy part."

I ran through the details of our plan—out of our rooms after last check once the final heel clomps fell silent, done, then gathering in the washroom to ready ourselves for slinking down the stairwell to the heavy metal door in the basement, done. The only concern was what we would say if caught. My heart lodged in my throat.

"Not a worry. I can cause a massive distraction if needed," Emma blurted out. "I don't give a goddamn what these bitches do to me. They'll never own me. I won't let them."

Kaitlin huffed. "Well, let's get it over with. We're only wasting time here."

We crept to the door, hesitantly peeking out. The coast was clear, and we darted through the hall to the end. Darkness in the stairwell spilled out, and we hid in the shadows of its shelter.

"This way." I ran down the stairs with quick, light steps. My adrenaline fueled every muscle, and it sent my brain into overdrive. All I could think about was freedom.

Freedom to think my own thoughts. Freedom to move where I wanted to go. Freedom to speak what was on my mind. With these girls, in this stairwell...I was free.

Tears pooled in my eyes as I descended the stairs with Kaitlin and Emma at my heels. Our heavy breath and light giggles filled the echoing darkness as we reached the bottom.

As I moved to the door leading into the basement, a strange flash of red letters filled my mind, like deja vu. Was it a warning? I searched my memory for their meaning, but I could only hear quiet pulses of sound. Voices. I couldn't be sure, but it sounded like a chorus of voices chanting, "Help us."

I looked back at the girls to see if they heard it, too, but they only waited for me to move forward. The voices quieted for a moment, but then there was a burst of sound in my skull. My eyes widened at the explosion when the voices commanded me to, "Run!"

"Shit," I hissed. I pressed my back against the wall, searching upward through the dark shaft of the stairwell.

"What's wrong?" Kaitlin followed my gaze up the stairs.

"I don't know," I murmured, straining to listen. "I just have the strangest feeling. Like we've done this before. Like this has already happened."

"Yeah. You're nuts," Emma stated. "Remember?"

Smirking, I opened the heavy door as quietly as possible. Before I could look into the corridor, a deep voice shattered my mind into obliterated fragments.

"Figures I'd bump into you here." Patrick propped his mop against the wall. Then his hand went to his chin as he watched Kaitlin and Emma emerge from the stairwell as well. "You're crazy," he exclaimed. "Like, the real deal."

I chuckled, knowing he wouldn't turn us in.

"Patrick, you need to help us," I whispered.

"No way in hell," he said. "I don't see you. I never saw you." He snatched up his mop to continue mopping the floor. "What the hell are you doing anyway? It's dangerous down here. I think it's goddamn haunted half the time." He glanced down the dark hallway. "Night duty is enough to make me lose my mind, but in this creepy place… Christ."

His eyes remained fixed on me.

"We heard about the tunnels," Emma interjected.

Patrick's spine straightened, eyes darting to the door Jeannie had shown me earlier. He fidgeted and pretended to look elsewhere, including up at the ceiling.

"I already know that's the door," I teased. "Have you ever been in there?"

"Fuck, no," he said. "Crazy shit goes on in there. I've heard screams in the night. I tell you, it's haunted."

"It's supposed to connect the wards," Emma said. "Is it true?"

He nodded. "Yeah. Originally for winters, I guess. To avoid staff having to go outside. And there are some storage vaults, I think. But it became too dangerous. Cave-ins and floods."

"We're going to Ward B," Emma blurted.

My eyes nearly burst out of my head. "We are not! Jesus, Emma."

Patrick slopped his mop into the bucket with a splash. "That would *truly* be insane. That's where the dangerous patients are. Like, the criminally insane." His eyes met mine. "Don't go there. Please."

"We're just checking it out," I assured him, side-eyeing Emma. "We won't go far. I just want to see if the legend is true. You wanna come with us?"

"Jesus, Grace." He hesitated as if considering it for a fleeting second. "I can't afford to lose this job. I'm supporting my mother and my little brother. They're counting on me."

Guilt washed over me for bringing him into our sinister plan.

"No, of course," I said. "You're right." Then I thought for a moment. "You can keep watch, though. Please. If someone comes looking for us, you can send them off our trail."

His lips pressed to the side in exaggerated thought. "Possibly." He smirked.

I sent him a warm smile, wondering what may have caused him to become the provider for his family at such a young age, and why he had such kind eyes. I pulled in a deep breath, then turned to the ominous, rusted door leading to the tunnels.

"This way," I said to the girls. "Thanks, Patrick."

"Follow the white pipes," he muttered.

I held up a hand. "What?"

"The white pipes running along the ceiling. You won't get lost if you keep to the white pipes." He reached for the bag hanging from his bucket. "And you'll need this." He pulled a black object from the bag. It had a large glass orb at the end.

I took the flashlight from him. Then he pushed his bucket further away from us and swiped his mop across the floor in big, wet motions.

"Let's go," Emma pressed. "Come on!"

We flew to the dark, isolated door to the tunnels—the burrows, as Jeannie called them. And then I remembered she had warned of gophers. The hairs on the nape of my neck stood up as I pulled on the door.

With a huge crack and creaking hinges, it opened just enough for us to squeeze through.

CHAPTER 11

T he click of the flashlight echoed deep within the dark passage, and its diffused light led the way. As we stepped further into the tunnel, a waft of damp, stale air blew at our faces. I turned the light toward the ceiling, spotting the pipes running straight into the darkness.

"Follow the white pipes," I said.

Sounds of dripping water and whirling air rushed around us as we hurried through the narrow corridor. A gradual slope took us deeper into the earth, and the temperature dropped with each passing step.

"This is creepy," Kaitlin whispered, clamping onto my arm. "What if someone's down here?"

"Doing what?" Emma interjected. "Devil worshipping? It's the middle of the night!"

"I know, but you never know," she mumbled.

I pushed through the shadows and thick must, feeling like no one had been down here in decades. But then a space opened at the end of the tunnel.

"There's something up ahead," I said, walking faster. "Like a room, I think."

We hurried through to the opening, and I shone my light all around.

"It's like a billiards hall," Emma sang.

I darted the light all around the large space. Emma was right, sort of, about the billiards. A pool table in the middle of the room had cues and balls strewn across it. Other items were tossed about—boxes, crates, and a table with the most amazing item sitting on it.

A record player!

It looked like one of the original phonographs, with a huge horn spiraling from the side. The newer models had sound that came from fabric at the front of the box. This was like the ones in magazines.

"A game room?" Kaitlin asked.

"I don't know," I said. "More like storage, I think." I fiddled with the lamp that was also on the table. When I yanked the chain, it buzzed to life. A line coming out of the wall connected to the lamp's worn cord. The gentle glow of light spread across the room, and I clicked off my flashlight.

Emma moved to the record player, then cranked the handle at the side. She lifted the needle, smiled, and placed it on the black disc that spun on the surface. In an instant, crackling sounds came out of the megaphone before it released the most beautiful sound.

Music.

Modern music.

A woman's voice broke in through the jazz piano. We all paused to listen to her.

"I was crazy 'bout a man…" Her raspy voice filled the room. "Mine, all mine…trouble, trouble." I swayed to her tale of a broken heart.

"Bessie Smith," Emma said with her eyes closed. "She's the queen of jazz." And she moved her body to the music in sensual waves.

Kaitlin held the wooden edge of the billiards table. In pace with the music, she ran her fingers over the intricately carved corner. A woven leather pouch sagged beneath the pocket, waiting to catch a masterfully shot billiard ball.

Then the hairs on my arms pricked up as the song continued. "Downhearted blues…" The words repeated over and over. "Downhearted blues." My ears began to burn as my heartbeat pounded in them.

Kaitlin's voice pulled my attention from the player as she pulled something white from the leather pouch at the corner of the billiards table.

"What the hell?" Her voice trailed off in confusion.

Instead of a cue ball, she pulled a small piece of lace-trimmed fabric from the pocket. When she shook it out, it became clear it was a woman's undergarment. Intimate undergarment.

"Panties?" Emma grabbed them for inspection. "What the fuck?"

I stared at the familiar lace trim. One I'd seen a dozen times whenever Jeannie arranged her night-time underwear with her pajamas before tucking them under her pillow in the mornings.

The song hit me between the eyes with its repetition. "Down-hearted blues..."

Vomit rose in my throat.

"Those are Jeannie's," I spat. "This is her song."

My eyes darted between Kaitlin and Emma. The underwear hung from Emma's fingers as she stared at me in disbelief.

"Well, someone's been fucking your poor Jeannie," Emma stated. "I'd say right about here." Her fingers trailed around white stains on the old felt of the table, like dried fluids of some kind.

My breath stopped short as Jeannie's words of warning exploded in my mind. "You'll get lost in there. You'll never come out the same." Someone had hurt her. "Don't go too far in," she had said. She was trying to protect me from similar abuse. "Beware of the gophers."

Kaitlin looked around the table for other clues, then bent and reached under it. She pulled a notepad and pencil out, then placed them on the red felt. She stepped back with a pale grimace so we could see her display.

She didn't need to say anything. We'd all seen that type of notepad and pencil before--pretentious and scholarly.

"The fucking shrink," Emma barked. "That pervert. Fucking a goddamn child." She grabbed a cue stick, then launched it across the room like a spear. "Can't keep his prick in his pants. Asshole."

It felt like my head was going to burst off my body. How could anyone want to hurt Jeannie? My nerves twitched as I confirmed Emma's accusation in my mind. I'd seen the notepads and the pencils in one place only. Dr. Kilbride's office.

The music stopped, and crackles popped out of the hissing megaphone.

"I need to get out of here." Kaitlin stepped away from the table.

Every muscle in my body wanted to run. My attention moved to the tunnel, then a whisper escaped my mouth. "Does anyone smell smoke?"

Emma threw the underwear into the corner as she bolted toward the door leading into the tunnels. Her nose lifted into the air, following the smell of the smoke.

"Wait!" Kaitlin's panicked voice pierced through the thick air.

I grabbed the flashlight, following Emma into the dark passage. She'd already traveled farther than I could see her, in the direction leading away from our ward.

"Emma, slow down," I called, sweeping my light through the darkness.

The smell of smoke grew stronger as I reached a turn in the tunnel. I slowed to allow Kaitlin time to catch up, then beamed my light around the corner.

Emma leaned with her back against the wall, one foot propped up behind her. A bright red glow lit up her face as she took a long drag from a cigarette.

Leaning toward a dark figure against the wall across from her, she blew her smoke into his face.

My flashlight shook in my hand, sending light bouncing through the tunnel in every direction. With two hands, I steadied the beam and shone it on his face.

"Grace," Emma said with a smirk. "Bobby found us."

Kaitlin raced up behind me.

94

"Shit!" Her voice shot out of her, almost sounding out of control. "We shouldn't be here. Let's go." She stepped backward.

"Hell no," Emma replied. "Not without a game first."

She turned the cigarette in her fingers, then placed it between Bobby's lips. Without lifting a hand, he puffed on the cigarette and took a long drag. His eyes held hers without flinching, and she giggled as he exhaled the smoke through his nose.

Feeling like I should turn my eyes away, I lowered the light. Kaitlin's grip on my elbow tightened, and I lifted the beam again.

My voice finally broke free. "How did you find us?"

Without taking his gaze off Emma, he replied, "The white pipes. They connect the wards."

I shot my light to the ceiling to confirm the pipes were still there. Bobby reached into his pocket, pulled out a metal cigarette lighter, and flicked it open. When he scratched it to life, a tall flame rose from his hand, lighting up the area around us.

"I keep it hidden in my jock," he said with a smirk. "Last guy who tried to search me there got a broken nose." He closed the lighter, the flame going dark. "They had me restrained for a week, but it was worth it."

"Assholes..." Emma purred like a graceful cat in his ear. "Come on. We'll show you what we found." She pulled him off the wall, then pushed past us. "Shine the light back to the room," she called to me.

Kaitlin and I followed as Emma pulled Bobby toward the game room.

"This is insane," Kaitlin whispered. "He's a goddamn murderer. A psychopath."

I aimed my beam on his back. "He seems kind of normal to me. Maybe he really didn't do it."

Kaitlin let out a sigh that cut me. Though it was too dark to see, I knew she was rolling her eyes.

The four of us followed the glow from the doorway, then spilled into the game room. I couldn't help but think of poor Jeannie. This room was her hell and I was determined to be sure she never entered it again.

The light from the lamp flickered and buzzed as Bobby brushed past it. He went straight for the billiards table, running his hands across the red felt.

"We had one of these at my fraternity house," he said as he reached into the pockets, pulling out billiards.

He made his way around the entire table, rolling colorful balls across the surface. Emma gathered two cue sticks, then handed one to him.

Keeping one eye glued to him, I flipped the records in the box near the player and pulled one out. Turning it over in my hands, I blew the dust off it and replaced Bessie Smith with the new record. After cranking the side handle, I lowered the needle on the spinning disc.

Crackling pops shot out of the megaphone, then sounds of big-band jazz. The smooth, crooning voice of a man filled the room. For a moment, we all felt...normal.

Bobby set the billiards in a triangle formation in the center of the table. Several balls were missing from the set, but he rejoiced in having found the white cue ball.

"Ladies first," he said to Emma, passing her the white ball.

Stepping closer to him, she bumped him aside with her hip. "Don't mind if I do."

She set the ball on the felt, leaning in with her stick. I nearly blushed as I watched her shimmy her hips when she prepared for the first strike. Bobby couldn't take his eyes off her.

Kaitlin finally moved in away from the door, approaching the record player. Her eyes continued to dart from Bobby to the door, as if she were calculating her exit route if he decided to try to massacre us on the spot.

"Find another good one." I motioned for Kaitlin to go through the box of records.

Swaying to the music, I moved around the player as if I had an invisible dance partner. Something about the music awakened a feeling of hope and joy within me. It was a feeling I hadn't known in such a long time—and one I never wanted to forget.

And the feeling of being with...friends. Of not being watched with critical glares at every moment. It was exhilarating.

But it was frightening at the same time. The fear of never feeling this again was more than I could bear.

I stood taller, promising myself I would get out of this place. I'd get us all out of this hellhole.

I turned to Bobby. "Do you ever think of breaking out?"

Lowering his stick, he took his eyes off Emma for the first time. He turned to me with an angry expression in his eye. "Every day," he said. "But where would I go? They think I'm a killer."

"None of us have anywhere to go," I replied. "But we still need to get out."

He banged the bottom of his stick on the ground, and I flinched. "I'd be shot on sight."

My eyes lowered from his as I considered his situation. It **was** different from ours. He was considered criminally insane while simple quackery and lust caused our incarceration.

Then he added, "But a bullet in the back as a free man would be better than this bullshit."

"Exactly," I said, meeting his eyes again.

Something in his gaze made me trust him. The youthful boyish glance. The innocence. It was so hard to believe he could have done what they said.

"You're the only ones in here who look at me like anything other than a crazed murderer." He turned his gaze back on Emma. "Well, you two anyway." Then he shot a quick glance at Kaitlin.

Kaitlin looked up from the record box, but she avoided his eyes. "I'm fine," she said. "I mean, you're fine."

We all burst out laughing at her nervous fumbling. For the first time, I watched her shoulders relax in his presence.

He lined his stick up for his next shot before addressing us again. "We should bring my buddies down here," he said. "They're a bit too proper for it, but I think they'd like the awkward appeal."

I remembered his college friends were coming to visit. From the outside.

97

My eyes widened with a new idea. "Do you think they could help us get out of here?"

～

Bobby balanced his chin on the top of his cue stick, considering my words. Maybe I was too quick to suggest his friends could help get us out of here. I barely knew him, but his friends were the only connection to the outside. They sounded like they were, well, *normal*.

"Believe me," he said. "I've been wondering the same thing." He cracked his stick against the cue ball, sending it smashing into a cluster of colorful balls. "My security guard is generally attached to my hip, when he's not passed out, that is, so conspiring a plan would be tough. He'll be listening to every word."

"Maybe on the court, you know, playing with the ball," I suggested. "He always stands off to the side when you're practicing."

He lowered his stick. "True." He pulled a fresh cigarette out of his shirt pocket, then placed it between his lips.

I watched him mulling over what I'd said. Just before I pulled my eyes away, Emma slinked over to him.

"Need a light?" she asked as she reached for the waistband of his pants.

He grabbed her wrist to stop her fingers from dipping underneath the band. His smile grew wide as he pulled the lighter from his groin area with his other hand. "Thanks, but I got it."

She plucked the lit cigarette from his mouth, then placed it in her own. Sucking on it with a sensual stare, she worked her mouth on the cigarette like it was something obscene.

He wrapped his arm around her waist, pulling her closer.

"Come here," he said, holding her against his body. "I want to show you something." He moved with her to the door, leading her out into the darkness of the tunnel.

Her giggles echoed through the maze of twists and turns, but the sound remained close enough we knew they hadn't gone far.

I grabbed onto Kaitlin, yanked her to the far side of the billiards table, and whispered, "I think he's the ticket for us getting out of here." My eyes widened with childlike hope. "Don't you see it? His friends. If we come up with a plan?"

"Grace," Kaitlin interrupted me. "We don't know them. And he's certifiable. I don't even think we should let Emma be alone with him right now." She glanced at the door, motioning to the sound of their mumbled voices.

My eyes dropped to the floor but then lifted again. "I know. But it's our only option right now. He's our only connection to the outside. We have to at least try."

The music seemed to get louder in my head as I allowed it to move through me. I reached for Kaitlin's hands, then whirled her around in circles. The more we spun, the wider her smile grew.

"Can't you feel it?" My head fell back as we twirled. "Our freedom."

Her hands held mine with more strength as her feet moved faster, spinning us in a blur of motion. Then, as the music slowed and then stopped, only crackling came from the megaphone and Kaitlin nodded at the player.

"Yeah," she said "I feel it. I didn't want to, though."

"Why?" I dropped her hands.

"Because now I won't be able to survive in there." Her eyes moved back to the door, toward the Excited Ward.

"Exactly." I smiled. "We can't lose that feeling, Kaitlin. Or they win."

"They've already won," she murmured.

"No. We are still us. I can feel it." I stood taller. "But we can't let them know that. We still need to act like conforming zombies. But we're busting out, Kaitlin. We're getting out of here to reclaim our lives."

With a stumbling crash, Emma and Bobby fell back into the game room, breathless. I averted my eyes, embarrassed, as if they needed more privacy.

A gentle grin decorated Bobby's face, and his lids hovered at half-mast. Emma moved straight for the record player to start it up again. She moved back to Bobby, settling into his embrace for a dance.

"We should probably get back," I said. "Before anyone notices we're gone."

Kaitlin cranked the handle on the record player to get the music started again.

"No…" Emma whined. "I want to stay here forever." Her eyes held Bobby's as if sealing a pact.

His arms closed around her waist, holding her tight. "Grace is right," he whispered to her. "We want to be able to do this again, right?"

Emma's bottom lip shot out in a pout, and he leaned down to kiss it.

Butterflies took flight in my stomach as I watched the caring exchange. His tender act proved to me he wasn't capable of what they had blamed him of. No one could do such a thing yet still have such affection for another person.

"Come on, Emma," I called. "We'll come back when Bobby's friends visit in a couple days. But we gotta go. Now."

Emma pulled away from Bobby without breaking eye contact, and he dropped his arms from her waist.

I clicked on my flashlight, then pulled the cord of the lamp to shut it off. We moved out of the game room into the tunnel, and Bobby scratched his lighter to life. He reached out to Emma for one last kiss before turning away, then jogged into the abyss of the tunnels. His light faded as he followed the white pipes and left our sight.

Emma's shoulders sank almost to the floor, and I took her arm to keep her from following him. "You'll see him again. I promise," I whispered as I tugged her to follow us.

Kaitlin led the way, running her hands along the sidewalls of the tunnel. The music grew quiet as we moved farther from the game room, then it ended altogether. The final notes resonated deep within me, solidifying my commitment to our escape.

"The door is up there," Kaitlin whispered. "You should leave the flashlight in here, so no one finds it."

I clicked the light off as she pushed the door open, and the dull beams of dawn's awakening filled the space with gray illumination.

We crept into the hall of the basement of the Excited Ward. I silently hoped Patrick would still be there, waiting for us. The handle of his mop leaned against the wall, out of its sloppy bucket, and I knew he couldn't be far off.

"What if they catch us before we get back to our rooms?" Kaitlin whimpered.

We snuck toward the stairwell. "We'll have to pretend we were…"

My words stuck in my throat as Patrick moved out of the stairwell into the corridor. Something about the expression on his face stopped my heart, and I froze.

Then, stepping out from behind him, Nurse Totten glared at us as the edges of her sinister grin lifted toward her piercing eyes.

CHAPTER 12

"Well, well, well. What have we here?" Nurse Totten sneered as her fingertips tapped against each other. "Lost church mice?"

The blood drained from my face. Kaitlin whimpered as she clamped onto my elbow.

Patrick shot a quick glance of apology at me, and his devastation poured from his pupils.

"It was my fault…" Emma's voice shattered the brittle stalemate. "They were only trying to help me." Her eyes begged us to play along. "I was feeling scared after a nightmare. I think I was sleepwalking."

"I see…" Totten's sour voice trailed through the silence of the basement as the wheels in her mind turned. "But still, no one should be out of their rooms at this hour. Unsupervised."

I silently prayed she didn't know where we'd been. It would ruin everything.

Totten's head shook in feigned disappointment. "Pity. I'd really hoped you all had learned your lessons. But sure, that would be too much to expect of the feebleminded." She turned to Patrick. "Did you have anything to do with this, young man? Choose your words carefully." She glared at him, waiting for a response.

My eyes shot wide, begging him to protect himself and his job.

"No, I've just been tending to my nightly tasks," he replied.

The shake in his voice was hard to miss. Totten wouldn't.

She searched his eyes, waiting for any additional clues to his involvement. "Well, we'll see." She stepped closer to him with a narrow squint, examining him.

He stepped back from her pressure, twitching with nervous jitters.

"We didn't even know he was here," I interjected, an edge to my voice I couldn't conceal.

Totten's head jerked around to me. "Trying to defend your boyfriend?" She prowled closer. "Your tone betrays you."

"He's not my boyfriend," I stated, recognizing too late I was falling into her trap.

"I see." She looked between Patrick and me. "Yet, you're quick to defend him."

"Can we just go back to our rooms?" Emma sighed.

Nurse Totten whirled on Emma. To Patrick, she snapped, "We'll see where your allegiance lies. Grab her. Help me to get her to the tub. Her disrespectful attitude requires a cleansing. As for the other two, time in solitary is needed for corrective measures."

Terror widened my eyes as nausea moved through me. The tub was barbaric. Some patients didn't survive it. They died of hypothermia or drowned. And the thought of another minute in solitary was enough to drive me over the edge.

Patrick froze in his place, refusing to follow her directive to grab Emma.

"Thought so." Totten grimaced. "I'll need additional reinforcements then. And you, sir, you'll be out on your tail by sunup."

My jaw fell as I stared at Patrick. Why had he done that? He should have just played along. But his eyes met mine with determination, expressing he'd done the right thing. Either way, my heart broke for him. He'd been caught in the middle, and I couldn't help but think it was my fault. I knew it was.

"To your rooms," she commanded. "Immediately." Her gaze pierced Patrick. "And you, sir, will be reported to the superintendent. Dr.

Johnson won't tolerate such defiance in his staff. He values order and subordination. You, my friend, have broken the code here."

Patrick's shoulders squared as he grew more confident in his determination. He nodded for me to get going to my room, so not to have her wrath focused back at me. The subtle interaction didn't go unnoticed by Totten, and her face reddened with anger.

"Do I note a conspiracy?" She shot a questioning glare at each of us. "One I must squash?" She shoved us toward the stairs. "Up. Now," she barked.

As the key turned in the lock of my solitary room, I ran at the door and pressed my face into the small cross-shaped window. One second. Two seconds. Three. Time was evil in solitary. It crept so slowly, allowing plenty of space for the demons to take over my mind.

"Stay focused, Grace," I spoke aloud. "Don't go to the dark places."

I rapped on the glass with my knuckles until Kaitlin appeared in her window across from me. Pointing two fingers to my eyes, I then aimed them at her, trying to convince her to stay with me—to stay focused. She nodded, but the terror in her eyes was impossible to miss.

Solitary had injured us before. It stole our souls. But each time, we healed. Maybe not as we once were, but we were able to find ourselves again in the mist and darkness. The worst fear was of hitting a point where we'd never find ourselves again. I refused to let that happen now. There was too much at stake. Our freedom loomed only days away.

I held Kaitlin's eyes with mine as I counted the days to Saturday and the scheduled visit with Bobby's friends. Straining to measure time, I figured it must be Thursday. If I fought to stay awake, I could measure the days with dusk and dawn, but that was the problem. Sleep was the only true escape from the torture of isolation. Without it, I'd feel every single lingering second.

Lifting my fingers to my window, I pressed three of them against the glass. Three days until Saturday. Kaitlin nodded with understanding, but her brows lifted in worry. And I held the same concern in my heart. What if we were in solitary for longer than three days? What if we missed the visit?

It was possible. There was no telling how long we'd been kept in solitary before. It felt like an eternity each time—long enough to lose our minds, swallowed by the terror of our own creeping, twisting thoughts.

I straightened, deciding to spend every waking moment planning our escape. If I could focus the time on a specific task, one that would deliver my freedom, then I surely wouldn't lose my mind this time. I prayed Kaitlin would use the same strategy.

Pressing my cheek against the window again, I glanced down the hallway to the next door. Typically, Emma's face would be in the next window, but there was no sign of her. As I studied the details of her door, I noticed a thin line of a shadow along the edge. It was open, which meant no one was inside.

Emma was somewhere else.

My stomach dropped. Totten had it out for Emma. Her punishment would be more severe. She had mentioned the tub to Patrick when he refused to help her with her punitive plans. If Emma was in water therapy, she'd be in serious danger. Totten's idea of water therapy had nothing to do with relaxation or calm. It had everything to do with freezing to death and oxygen-deprivation therapy. She said the cold and near-drowning cleansed the demons and created a desirable tranquility. I was no medical doctor, but I was fairly sure the lack of oxygen to the brain could cause permanent damage—enough to subdue a patient. Forever.

My heart pounded in my ears. Helplessness washed over me as I pulled on my locked door. Begging for release, I smashed my hands on the glass window. But no one came. No one cared.

Sobbing, I fell into the rear corner of my tiny room. It was so unfair. Our lives were being stolen right from our hands. And we couldn't do anything about it from here.

My hands covered my face as I spiraled into helpless insanity.

Layers of my personality ripped away, exposing my purest form. My true nature. She was vulnerable without the armor of my day-to-day existence, but she was strong at the same time. Her mind was clear. Her spirit powerful.

But she was frightened.

Her memories flashed through her mind until they ran out. But they didn't stop there. They blasted further, showing memories that hadn't happened yet. Flashing through future events.

I pressed my head against the wall, my eyes popping open in terror. Not able to stop the images from unfolding before me, I cried out to make it stop.

Emma's face shattered my mind. Horrified, I stared into her fogged-over eyes as she swung by her neck from a tree.

Pulling on my hair, I struck my head against the wall, over and over, trying to make the racing visions stop. My body jolted and I kicked against the floor, pushing myself into the wall as hard as I could. But nothing would stop the prophetic images. They played through my mind like a cinema show that refused to end.

Collapsing in exhaustion, my limbs splayed under me. Weakly, I laid there, panting. Without energy to continue fighting, the images came to full life and I fell victim to watching them once again.

Emma's body hung lifeless from a rope around her neck. She twisted on the end of it, every detail of her unfair death on display. Her bloated purple face emanated vengeance. She'd held the final power, had the last word. She'd made the ultimate choice. And she'd died in control of her own destiny.

It was no surprise. She would never let anyone else make the decision for her.

Tears trailed down my face as I watched the next events unfold.

We'd known something was wrong, so in the visions we had searched for Emma. Kaitlin and I found her hanging from the tree. We grabbed onto her body, lifting it to release the tension on her neck, but it was too late. Our wails woke the entire asylum, and people came running from every direction.

The blur of panic surrounded us, and the crowd pushed us away from our friend. My mind's eye moved from the chaos to focus on the one thing that wasn't in a frenzy.

Bobby.

He stood at the fencing of his basketball court, staring at the sight of Emma's lifeless body. His expression moved from shock to rage. Bobby stepped back as if trying to find his balance. He looked in every direction, desperate for something to change what he'd seen, something to wake him up or snap him out of it. But his eyes kept returning to her swinging body, and I saw the moment the truth destroyed him.

He transformed from the lovestruck boy I'd known into a wild beast. His growls filled the air, and everyone turned to him.

"You killed her," he screeched. "You fucking psychos! You're the ones who should be locked up!" His voice pierced my soul with its angst.

He staggered around the court like a caged animal, panting and gasping for air. His hands ripped through his hair in anguish.

"Fucking psychos," he cried out.

His guard kept his distance on the outside of the fencing by the locked gate. He gripped the key in a tight fist, but the fear in his eyes proved he had no intention of opening the gate any time soon.

"You're worse than my fucking parents," Bobby yelled. "They had it coming just as you do!" Sobbing, he knelt over with his hands on his knees. Raising his head again, he almost howled his next words. "You can only torture someone for so long before they snap."

He lifted upright, looking directly at me. His head tipped to the side as if he'd had a thought. Or more like he came to a decision.

In that instant, he reached into his pants and pulled out his metal cigarette lighter. Before I could call out to him, begging him not to, he unscrewed the fluid chamber and doused himself with most of it. He then scratched the lighter into flame, lifted his foot and lit the cuff of his pants on fire. Within seconds, flames engulfed his clothing with a roar of a lapping inferno. The anguished boy stretched his arms out as if to invite the pain. His head fell back in visible rejoice as he burned right before our eyes.

In a black cloud of smoke and dancing orange flames, he collapsed, motionless, and lay smoldering on the court.

"No..." I screamed. "No! No! No!"

I ran toward him, knowing it was too late, and smashed into the wall of fencing. Stumbling back, I shook my head to clear it. The cross-shaped window of my silent prison stared back at me.

I gasped at the sudden change of scenery. Maybe it wasn't too late. There might still be time to stop the horrific events from unfolding.

"Let me out of here," I screamed. "They're going to die!"

CHAPTER 13

The sealed door to my solitary room flew open, and I fell out into the hall. My limp body splatted onto the floor in exhaustion as a black shoe kicked at my side.

"Get up. Time for breakfast," a cold voice barked.

The black shoes clomped to the door across from mine, and the person pulled it open as well. I lifted my head enough to look in.

"Kaitlin," I whimpered through a dry, scratchy throat.

She cowered in the far corner without lifting her head.

"Kaitlin," I called again with a squeak. "Come out. Please."

"Ach, fer the love o' Christ, get moving, girl." Nurse Totten's voice sent rage through my veins as her black shoe tapped with impatience.

The anger was enough to lift me to my feet, and I stood tall with clenched fists.

"Don't be lookin' so confident, or I'll have you back in solitary before your next breath," Totten spat.

My mind swam with ways to suppress her— running tackle, smashing her head into the floor, dragging her into a solitary room and throwing away the key. But no. I wouldn't lower myself to her level. There would be another way for vengeance. A more civilized— or sane—means. So for now, my focus had to remain on getting out of solitary and regrouping with Kaitlin and Emma. It was clear to me this would be our last chance.

Lowering my eyes, I waited for Totten's next command. Kaitlin crawled out of her room into the hall, then clutched my ankles. Crouching to her level, I reached under her shoulders and pulled her up.

"It's okay, Kaitlin," I whispered. "You're safe now. We're together again."

She whimpered like a frightened child.

My teeth clenched, and I fought to keep my blaming glare off Totten. Instead, I focused on helping Kaitlin. She hadn't had the same distraction of prophetic visions to keep her occupied while imprisoned in solitary, and I worried for her mental stability. At the same time, I held on to the images that had presented themselves to me in my room and believed every snapshot.

Kaitlin's head fell onto my shoulder as I supported her weight and dragged her along with me. We followed Totten to our rooms where the other girls were getting ready for breakfast.

"Don't leave me," Kaitlin begged as her fingernails dug into my arm.

"I won't," I assured her. "Just grab the fresh frock on your bed, and we can get ready together in the washroom."

We stumbled through the process of washing the filth of solitary off our bodies and replenishing with clean frocks. It was the first step at recovering from the trauma that left us shell-shocked.

Roaming like unconscious zombies, we followed the other girls to the dining hall. As we staggered in the line, I realized my traumatized state was halfway an act. Somehow, while in solitary, my mind had been so active, I didn't have the typical psychological symptoms of barbaric isolation. In fact, I felt stronger in my mind than ever—ready to pounce.

Unfortunately, the same wasn't true for Kaitlin and she needed my help to recover her broken spirit.

I inhaled my flavorless porridge like a starved animal while Kaitlin dipped her spoon in and out of the bowl.

"You have to eat, Kaitlin," I encouraged. "It's necessary for getting strong again. You can do this."

Her eyes lifted slightly, then shifted to motion behind me.

Betty leaned over from the other table, then tapped my shoulder. Her kind eyes met mine with concern. I couldn't imagine how she had it in her to offer support to others. I suppose she was the mother figure in here, as if needing to redirect her maternal instinct somewhere.

"Emma's still in The Hole," she whispered, shooting a hawk's eye around the room to be sure we weren't being watched.

"What?" I seethed. Though my intuition screamed it was the only place she could be.

"I heard Nurse Totten bragging to the night staff about the length of time she kept her in the tub." Her eyes remained averted from mine, and her voice dropped to a low hush. "Said she had to break her strong will."

"My God. She'll kill her." I choked on my words.

"I can't stand to see any of you girls hurt," she murmured, shaking her head. "My son was the same age when I...lost him." Her eyes misted. "The war took so much from us. And without him, I had no purpose. No reason to live. But you girls, with all the life you have... you give me new hope."

A gentle smile lifted the edges of my mouth. No wonder she was like a mother to us. Always giving the supportive nod or a tender touch on the shoulder. Motherhood didn't leave when a child did. It remained. And hers...it festered with nowhere to go, landing her in this insanity. At least her instinctual mothering now had focus.

"I'm going to get her out of there," I whispered to Betty, grateful for the information she gave to me.

"Be cautious," she added. "Nurse Totten is on a warpath for the three of you. Says you're disrupting the order of the institution." Her head shook. "It's not good. I've seen what she's capable of." Her eyes fell on the table at the back—the one with the silent patients, some drooling, others staring at nothing. "I don't want any of you to end up in the Quiet Ward."

A shiver ran up my spine, and the jolt snapped Kaitlin to awareness.

"What about the Quiet Ward?" Kaitlin interjected.

"Nothing," I quickly replied. "Just chatting."

"No, stop trying to protect me." Her voice grew louder. "Is Emma in the Quiet Ward?"

Kaitlin's new vigor widened my eyes with hope.

"No. Keep your voice down." I nudged her ribs. "She's in The Hole."

"All this time?" she screeched.

"Quiet, Kaitlin!" I shot my stern tone through clenched teeth. "We'll figure it out when we leave here. There are too many eyes and ears on us. Just eat your breakfast."

She scooped her spoon into her porridge, then shoveled a heaping pile into her mouth. My air released in a long exhale I'd been holding in for all of breakfast. Kaitlin was returning, and it was the focus of saving Emma that would bring her back quickly.

I turned back to Betty. "What day is it?"

Pity filled Betty's eyes, like I was a lost sheep. But none of that mattered. I just needed to know the day. If we'd missed the visit from Bobby's friends, we'd be back to zero.

Her head tipped to the side. With a gentle nod, she whispered, "Saturday."

My heart caught in my throat as Betty mouthed the word, "Saturday." Bobby's friends would be arriving at some point, and we couldn't lose this opportunity. Emma was still gone, but Kaitlin and I could meet up with them to form a plan of escape.

After clearing our table, we filed out of the dining hall in line with the other girls. Totten led from the front, and the newer training nurses staggered their positions at various points near patients who appeared to require assistance.

Something was different, though. A strange silence surrounded me, and I looked all around. And there, at the fencing around the court, Bobby stood within, pressing his face against the chain link.

His eyes hooked onto mine, and he gave a subtle nod. I nodded back in agreement of our plan to meet up later tonight. But then his eyebrows pulled together as he searched the line for Emma. He looked at me questioningly. I dropped my gaze and turned away, not knowing how to tell him or even if I should.

"He knows," Kaitlin murmured. "I can tell. He knows something's up."

"Yeah," I agreed. "He's not stupid. We've been gone for two days, and Emma's still missing. He knows something's not right."

"What do we do?" Kaitlin glanced back at him.

I thought about arriving in the tunnels to meet the boys—without Emma. It would be terrible. Bobby's disappointment would shatter me.

"We have to get Emma out before tonight," I said as we filed into the ward.

Kaitlin slowed her pace. Her head shook. "I can't get punished again, Grace. I can't."

My eyes closed as her words weighed on me. "I know. But Kaitlin, it's our last chance," I said.

"What do you mean?"

"If we don't get out of here...if we don't get Emma out..." I stuttered on my words. "Kaitlin, I saw stuff when we were in solitary. Like, seeing events that haven't happened yet."

Kaitlin froze in her tracks, her eyes glazing over. Then, through trembling lips, she said, "Me, too."

"Wait! What did you see?" I stopped short as the other girls passed around me to move up the stairwell.

"It was you and me. But like, in a different time. Our clothes were strange, and we looked like we were from another place." She glanced around before speaking again. "We were trapped in the ward, and we couldn't get out. They'd boarded it up from the outside. Every window. Every door."

My hand flew to my mouth. I'd seen that vision, too, at some point.

Maybe in a dream. But she was right. They'd trapped us within a condemned building. The ruins of the Excited Ward. The images of peeling paint, shuttered windows, and dripping pipes shook me to my core.

"I saw Emma," I mumbled.

"Hanging from a tree?" Kaitlin finished my thought.

I grabbed onto her hand. "What is happening? We're having the same dreams?"

"It's like it's all happened before. It makes no sense," she whimpered.

"And I saw Bobby," I added.

"What about him?"

"I'm not sure. But it was like he...like he blamed them for killing her. And it wasn't his fault for killing his parents. And then he..." I fell silent, remembering the horrific sight of the flames. "He killed himself."

Tears filled Kaitlin's eyes as her hands trembled. "It's happening, Grace. It's like a prophecy foretelling the future. The ward is doing this. It's making us all crazy." She fidgeted and twitched. "We're actually going crazy."

"No." I yanked on her hand to snap her out of her growing hysteria. "We're not the crazy ones." I glanced at Nurse Totten as she commanded the girls into the laundry area. "They are."

I pushed my wooden pole into the vat of sloppy laundry, then stirred the stew of frocks in the gray water. My mind raced far beyond the cold, wet tubs as I ran through ideas of how to rescue Emma, each one sending me down darker rabbit holes.

Glancing across the dirty suds, I caught Kaitlin's gaze. She stared at me with a resolve I hadn't seen in her for some time. And it was clear. She was ready to make a move.

My heart rate accelerated as I shot my eyes to each nursemaid keeping watch on the room. There was no way to sneak out without being stopped or questioned. The blood drained from my face as I panicked at the thought of a lost opportunity.

A slop of wetness hit my ankle as a cold frock splatted on the floor next to me. When I looked up, I caught Betty staring at me with a grin as her pole hovered in the air like a freshly cast fishing pole.

I studied her face, wondering if she'd lost her mind, but then she reached her pole back into her tub and pulled out another frock. She whirled the end of her stick, slinging the saturated frock at Jeannie. The wet mass slapped her on the cheek, and she screamed.

Before Jeannie's affronted cries reached the nursemaids, Betty's pole was back in the vat, fishing out another frock. And splat! A wet mass sprayed across the room, then landed on the new girl's shoulder. Picking it off herself like it was a poisonous jellyfish, the girl held the soggy garment between her fingers and flung it toward Betty.

Jeannie continued to sulk as Betty pulled another from the water and threw it across the room. Streams of water splashed across the girls, and they squealed with excitement. Within seconds, the girls used their own poles to lift garments out and fling them in every direction. Screams filled the room as the nursemaids ran inside to regain order.

The youngest nursemaid, trying to prove her worth, ran for Betty, only to slip in the muck and slide into a brimming vat. She fell over the edge, soaking her sleeves. Her tiny, square cap fell off her head into the putrid scum.

I launched toward Kaitlin. Pulling her from the chaos, I yanked her straight out the door and closed it behind us.

"Betty just bought us our chance!" I exclaimed. "Come on. Let's not waste it!"

We ran down the hall to the nurses' station. I hurried inside, searching for the wooden box that hid the keys to the doors and, more importantly, The Hole. But I couldn't find the box anywhere. I checked the walls for hooks and pulled the desk drawers open, searching for any sign of them.

"They're not here," I called to Kaitlin.

"Get out of there before someone comes."

I stepped out into the corridor, my body moving straight for the stairwell. "Come on. We need to go to her. To at least let her know we're trying."

Kaitlin turned toward the laundry room, making sure the door was still closed. Muffled sounds of playful screaming and stern commands from the nurses traveled to us, pushing us toward the stairs.

Without further hesitation, Kaitlin joined me and launched into the stairwell. We flew down the stairs to the first floor, stole through the halls toward the front lobby like church mice, then crept into the shadows of the alcove that hid the door to The Hole.

Kaitlin's eyes widened as she realized where the door led. Listening for any sign of staff, I pulled the door open and we snuck in. The sound of my pounding heart filled my ears as we hurried past the first door to the suitcase room to stop at the door to The Hole.

"Is this it?" Kaitlin's voice stuck in her throat as she tried to swallow.

I nodded, pressing my ear to the door.

"Emma?" I whispered. "Emma. It's us. It's me and Kaitlin."

A bang came from the room, like the sound of her heel hitting on the metal table. Sadness washed over me as I pictured her strapped to the cold examination slab. Then blazing anger replaced it as I vowed to bring justice to us all.

Her voice echoed within the damp space. "Grace…"

"Emma!" Kaitlin called.

"We're here," I said. "But I don't have the key." I jiggled on the handle of the door, but it remained solid in its locked housing. "We can't find it, Emma. But we'll keep searching. We'll get you out of there."

"The ward doesn't want it," she mumbled from within.

"What?" I pressed my ear harder against the door. "What did you say?"

"Don't you feel it?" Her voice held no emotion. "The ward owns your soul. It owns all of us. We're trapped here. Forever."

I looked at Kaitlin in confusion. The fear in her eyes chilled me as it proved her belief in Emma's words.

Emma continued in a monotone. "It's a cycle. See? Trapped on a hamster wheel. Racing around and around...around and around... around and around."

Twisting the handle of the door back and forth, I pushed my weight against it, trying to burst through. Emma had been in isolation for too long. Her mind wasn't coherent.

Her voice traveled out to us again, and I stopped my banging. "The ward spans time. Past, present, future. It's all the same here. Just different layers." She inhaled loudly as if in awe. "You know, being crazy isn't all that bad." She paused. "It's a gift really. One that lets you see the truth."

"Emma!" I called. "Keep focus on getting out of there. We'll find someone who can help. We'll get you out really soon."

"Grace," she called to me with a lucidity that hadn't been present in her other words. "Don't tell Bobby."

"Why not?" I spoke into the seam of the door. "He'll need an explanation of where you've been."

"I don't want him to get in any trouble," she stated. "He's been through enough. Please. Help me protect him." Her voice trembled with the request.

I glanced at Kaitlin. We'd hopefully be seeing Bobby tonight. The plan was to have freed Emma by then. At this point, I wasn't so sure it would be possible.

I pressed my lips back to the seam of the door to speak to Emma again, then terror shot through me as the door above opened with a jerk.

"Shit!" Kaitlin whimpered. "Someone's coming."

I grabbed onto her hand, snatching her away from Emma's door and into the suitcase room to hide. If it hadn't still been unlocked from my prior visit, we would have been discovered instantly.

Pressing my ear against the door, my breathing stopped as the loud clomp of hard-heeled shoes moved past our hiding place. A moment later, the jingle of keys and then the foul voice.

CHAPTER 14

Nurse Totten's callous voice bounced off the earthy walls of the dark basement as Kaitlin and I cowered. She'd jingled the keys, taunting me with why I couldn't find them in the nurses' station, and then pushed Emma's door open with a bang.

"Have we learned any manners yet?" Her voice sank into the oblivion of The Hole. "Had some time to repent?"

The sound of tin bowls clanging together gave me the opportunity to open the door of our hiding place to peek out. Totten had left a tray of water and a bowl of old, congealed porridge on the table just outside Emma's door. Her nasty voice trailed out again, causing my teeth to clench.

"Sure, you're too far gone to learn at this stage. Batty, you are," she taunted Emma. "Pity, really. Such a waste. Not much to be done though for the simpleminded."

Her cold, abusive tone curled my hands into fists.

"Come on," Kaitlin said. "Now's our chance to get out of here."

She was right. If caught, we'd be no help at all. But it killed me to think of leaving Emma down here with that evil woman. But then her voice cut through the dank air like a swiping sword.

"Yes. Pity, really," Emma retorted. "But nice they allow a place for the simpleminded to work. Nurse, they call you. Right? Seems you've taken nicely to the farce."

With that comment, I grabbed Kaitlin and we flew up the stairs. Totten would rage now at Emma's insolence. But she had no hope of breaking Emma's spirit. It was far too strong and had her beat.

As we tore through the halls toward the laundry, my heart sank as I thought of the additional hurt Emma had just brought upon herself. She'd get none of the curdled porridge. No water. Tighter straps. All of which made her rescue even more critical.

We snuck into the laundry and dropped to our hands and knees along with the other girls, mopping up the mess with a pile of dirty frocks. I crawled through the maze of clean-up, over to Betty.

"Thank you for the masterful distraction," I whispered.

Betty's face lit up with a broad smile.

"We found her. But she's still trapped in there," I added.

"Dear God." Betty exhaled with frustration.

Our attention shot toward the door then, as the nursemaids called for us to line up. Each holding a heavy basket of damp garments, we trailed down the stairs and out the ward.

We gathered at the clotheslines along the side of the building and set up to hang the frocks in the wind. With growing intensity, an incessant pounding drew my attention across the green.

There, standing in the court, was Bobby, bouncing his basketball with a loud, steady beat. His security guard stood tall by the locked gate. Once Bobby had my attention, he shot the ball toward the shadows within the fencing. In that same moment, two young men stepped into view, one holding the ball. When Bobby gestured to them, they focused on us.

"Kaitlin." I jabbed at her. "It's Bobby's friends. They're here."

She straightened, pushing the creases out of her frock.

I lifted a hand to wave to them.

His friends returned the motion as Bobby nodded agreement of our silent pact—meeting after midnight in the tunnels.

We'd decided on the time and place with full intention of having Emma with us. Now, I suddenly felt vulnerable and awkward without her. She was the one who made me feel comfortable around Bobby. Her heightened level of crazy was the perfect ice breaker. But now, I was on my own. Well, with Kaitlin.

I couldn't imagine how Bobby would get his friends into the tunnels. His security guard never took his eyes off him, but I figured, if he made it out the other night, he'd probably figure it out again. His guard couldn't be on him every second and apparently, according to Bobby, he had a drinking problem. Bobby had no qualms about using that caveat to his advantage.

It certainly explained how he could get into the tunnels at night, but what about his friends? He'd seemed so confident that they would be able to join him.

Then it occurred to me. There must be another entrance into the secret tunnels, accessible from outside of the wards. It was the only explanation. Maybe there was a separate access point for maintenance facility workers to use. My adrenaline coursed through my veins as I allowed myself to believe for a micro-second that maybe our rendezvous would work.

By dinner, there was still no trace of Emma. Judging by Totten's smug grin and quiet humming, Emma was likely not getting out any time soon.

"We have to tell Bobby where Emma is," I told Kaitlin as we made our way to the art room after our end-of-day meal of boiled ham and cabbage.

"I know. But she begged us not to."

Exhaling loudly, I thought about Emma's words. Her tone. And butterflies in my stomach took flight. She was protecting him. With her own suffering. The thought shot me in the heart as I realized what it was.

"It seems like...you know...like she loves him," I muttered.

Kaitlin halted in her tracks. "I had the same thought," she gasped.

"It's like there's a powerful connection between them. Like, unstoppable. Unbreakable."

"Exactly." I hesitated, thinking back to the way he looked at Emma, the way he touched her. "I don't know how he'll react to this. He's not exactly the most stable guy."

Kaitlin's eyes widened, clearly considering his past and the alleged action that got him locked up. "What do we do?"

"First, we need to worry about getting to the billiards room. That's our first hurdle. Then we figure it out from there."

I faced my blank canvas, rolling my eyes at the thought of having to create something in order to avoid a corrective lecture from the staff. They even treated the older women like children in here, never allowing free thought or the ability to make their own decision. The staff had clearly figured out how to the keep the Excited Ward subdued.

And in an instant, Totten's commanding voice shattered the dull balance. My eyes shot up and I stared at her imposing form in the doorway, pointing directly at Kaitlin and me.

"I want to see those two in the hall, immediately," she boomed.

Jeannie whimpered, then sank under her easel as Totten's voice soured the entire room. Betty's eyes shot to mine in alarm, and she stared in terror as Kaitlin and I stood up from our seats. Tilly began rocking in her chair, grabbing at her hair. As her voice grew into a scream, the nursemaids ran to her side to attempt to deescalate her episode.

The reaction of the girls in the room to Nurse Totten's command sent additional layers of panic through my muscles, and I struggled to move toward the door. Kaitlin stumbled after me as we walked toward our doom.

"Out!" she fired at us, pointing to the hallway.

We stepped out of the art room, certain we would face a firing squad in the corridor.

She stepped closer to us, forcing us against the far wall. Her foul breath filled our personal space. "I've had enough of your troubles around here, missies. And it's time something's been done about it." She scoured us with a turned lip, like we were vermin. "I've ordered a visit from Dr. Kilbride. He'll be evaluating you for..." Her voice trailed into the dark recesses of my mind as the psychiatrist's name shot jolts of terror through me.

I thought back to Jeannie's undergarments in the tunnel. And his misguided notes in our files of ridiculous diagnoses and treatments. He was a demon who worked for the ward. His aim was to please the ward and collect his paycheck. A chill ran through my veins.

My vision blurred as nausea threatened to drop me to my knees. "Please. It was all just a misunderstanding. We follow the rules here. We stick to our chores." I pleaded with her.

"Maybe so," she grunted. "But you don't choose your friends wisely. She's taken you down a misguided path. One the feebleminded can't navigate on their own. You'll be requiring Dr. Kilbride's assistance." She smirked. "Be ready first thing in the morning for your evaluations."

And she clomped away down the hall with a satisfied lift in her step.

My heart plummeted to my feet as Kaitlin's voice dug at me.

"What will...how will we...what will he...." Her terror caused incoherent speech.

It was true. We were in grave danger now. I knew it was wishful thinking to believe our punishment in solitary was the end of it. After Totten's visit with Emma this morning, she must have realized she required more torture to satiate her own writhing soul.

"We need help, Kaitlin," I gasped through my closing windpipe. "Like, real help."

I closed my eyes, searching my mind for anyone who could help us. Patrick's face filled my head, but he was gone. Totten had been rid of him swiftly. All that remained of his memory was the grimy mop, propped against the wall by the washrooms.

I missed his friendly, handsome face. It was the only thing that brought a piece of true reality into the ward. Rational thought, too. My heart squeezed tight from his absence and his inability to help us now. Because he would have. Without a second thought.

"Don't panic." I encouraged Kaitlin to return to the art room. "We'll figure this out. I swear."

She bit her nails to the quick as we sat at our canvases.

Betty glanced over at me. "What's happening?"

"It's okay." I gave a weak smile. "We're okay."

My words were as much for me as they were for her, to convince myself we would be okay. And with a deep inhale, I believed them.

I kept focus on what we needed to do next, and that was meeting up with Bobby and his friends to figure out our next steps. And Totten's threats weren't about to stop my plan.

The bright crescent moon took its sweet time passing across my window as I waited for its indication of midnight. Once it was out of sight, I knew it would be time to move.

The minutes passed like hours, but then, with the moon gone now, time jumped into overdrive. In a swift motion, I popped out of bed. I crept to the door, then pulled it open in slow motion. Peeking back to be sure I hadn't disturbed my roommates, I locked eyes with Jeannie.

She stared at me like I was a criminal and lifted her bear up to her face. I pressed my knees together, bouncing in a slight squat to show her I had to go to the bathroom. With a nod of understanding, she pressed her bear's ear into her mouth and snuggled deeper into her bed.

I slipped out of my room, then scurried toward Kaitlin's door. Hovering just outside it, listening for any rustling, I nearly peed myself from my twitching nerves. Then, with a click, Kaitlin was out of her room.

Running on tiptoes, we flew through the corridor and down the stairs. The gentle glow of flickering nightlights illuminated our way, but it tweaked my nerves with the haunting luminosity.

"Do you think they'll be there?" Kaitlin whispered as we entered the basement hallway.

I glanced both ways to be sure no one was down there with us, then snuck toward the door to the tunnels.

"I hope so," I said. "And I pray Patrick's flashlight is still there... or we'll be traveling through that place by sense of touch."

Kaitlin's face fell as I heaved on the door. It creaked open with loud resistance, and a fear of discovery made my muscles tense.

With only a few inches to squeeze through, we shimmied our way in. Light followed us from the hall, leading me to the flashlight that waited in the same spot I'd left it. Kaitlin closed the door behind us as gently as possible, but it still found a way to send booming echoes deep within the tunnels.

We froze without breathing, waiting for hidden assailants or booby traps to erupt. But only silence moved through the darkness.

I clicked the flashlight on, beaming it into the depths of the long tunnel.

"Let's go," I said. "We just follow the white pipes." I hoped our familiarity with the area would add a sense of security to our mission.

It was different without Emma. She was our free-spirited courage, the one who never second-guessed a thing. And that was exactly what we needed in this lonely depth of hell.

We made our way through the twists and turns of the cold underground corridor, keeping an eye out for the opening to the billiards room.

"I don't remember it being this far," Kaitlin squeaked.

"Yeah. Me too. I thought...wait." I shone the light at a sharp turn in the passageway. "Isn't that where Emma found Bobby? I think we passed the game room."

I turned and pushed past Kaitlin. Trailing my hand along the wall, I stopped short when I felt the outline of a door.

"This is it," I gasped. "I don't remember closing it, I guess."

I turned the old brass knob and pushed. Pitch darkness in the room sent chills through me, and I lifted the flashlight just as its light began to fade. I hit the side of the metal casing, then shook it. The beam grew stronger for an instant before dimming again.

"Quick," I instructed. "Flick on the lamp before it dies completely."

Kaitlin jumped toward the table with the lamp, bumping into the record player. As she pulled the cord, the light of the lamp buzzed to life with a flicker. At the same time, a crackling sound popped from the megaphone of the record player, making us jump like skittish animals.

I turned to Kaitlin with a nervous laugh. Then, out of the dark corner of the room, a voice pierced straight through my heart.

"What took you so long?"

The words bounced in my skull like ricocheting shrapnel, and I shook my head to clear it. As my sanity returned, I focused on Bobby's smiling face. His two friends stepped out of the darkness behind him.

"Where's Emma?" He glanced around us, eyeing the empty doorway.

I swallowed hard, trying to clear away the terror sweeping through me from their unexpected presence.

"They wouldn't let her out," I said. "They're keeping her on strict lockdown."

Disappointment oozed from his falling expression as his shoulders sank.

I'd promised Emma I wouldn't tell about her true situation, so I left out the gruesome details. But still, Bobby's crushed response proved he knew something was wrong. His hand ran over his face, then pressed his fingers over his eyes.

His friends moved closer to him, watching his response with concerned expressions. They knew he was hurting and wanted to help.

I took a step forward, wanting to help, too. I knew it would devastate Bobby to not see Emma, but nothing prepared me for the sadness that filled his eyes. His friends looked to me as if I had the answer.

"Hi," I said. "I'm Grace. This is Kaitlin." I gestured toward her as she kept a safe distance by the record player.

"Hi," the tall one replied. "I'm Brian. This is Nate."

I reached over, shaking each of their hands. A warm sensation travelled up my arm. There was something kind and familiar about the two of them, like I'd met them before at some point, but I couldn't place it.

"I guess it hasn't worked out as planned," I mumbled. "I'm sorry."

Brian reached his arm around Bobby's shoulder, then gave it a shake. "Next time, soldier." He attempted to lighten Bobby's mood. "Let's at least use this time, without any guards up your arse, to have a bit of fun."

He rolled the billiards toward the center of the table, then searched for the white one. "Nate, get some music going, will ya?" he called to his friend.

Nate moved toward the player, and Kaitlin stepped back. Then, after a friendly smile from him, she moved closer and showed him to the box of records.

I stepped up to Bobby. "We'll get her here next time. I promise."

He placed a cigarette between his lips, rolling it around. "Or not," he murmured.

My eyebrows pulled together as I studied his face.

He continued, "She's too smart for them. They won't allow it." He pushed a hand into his pants and pulled out his lighter. "She and I… we're not different. Punished for the crimes of others. Forced into decisions that cause us pain. We're just their pawns." He took a deep drag off his cigarette, the end glowing bight orange in the flame of the lighter.

'What do you mean?" I pressed.

"What I mean is…" His voice grew angry. "They're the crazy ones. Like my parents. Abuse. Neglect. Always pushing, pushing, pushing." He blew smoke at the ceiling. "They think we won't snap. But they're wrong."

My heart pounded in my chest as Bobby rambled on in his incoherent rant. He spoke of having no choice. He said he and Emma were one and the same. Both put in situations that twisted their destinies beyond recognition.

With each passing word, his face reddened further with rage.

Brian stepped in front of him, redirecting Bobby's attention to the stick in his hand. "You first. Break." He stepped aside, clearing Bobby's way to the red felt table.

Bobby's shoulders relaxed as he followed Brian's direction. A few strikes later, the game had his focus.

"It's like that time when we celebrated after the big game," Brian said while poking Bobby with his cue stick. "You shoot basketballs better than billiards." He chuckled.

Bobby sneered. "And you shoot billiards better than whiskey."

"Ooh, that's low," Nate chimed in. He leaned toward Kaitlin and said, "He can't hold his whiskey. Bobby'll never let him live it down."

Brian cracked the cue ball into a group of colorful ones. "You got me there. But I've come a long way since then. Give a guy a break."

"Yeah. Break me out of here," Bobby added.

Brian dropped his gaze. "I want to, my friend. We'll figure it out." He glanced up at me. "He doesn't belong here. None of you do."

I nodded and then looked away. I couldn't help but worry about Emma. "Yeah," I added. "I'm with Bobby. It's time to take the control back."

Bobby and his friends puffed out their chests in a hooting chant from their college. Kaitlin and I cracked up at their juvenile antics.

We watched the young men play together. Their jokes and jests pulled more old stories and memories out of them as they reminisced about their days at university. Nate added humorous details as Kaitlin giggled at the funny stories. The friendship between the boys was strong and real. It was clear Brian and Nate would do anything for Bobby, including getting him out of this hellhole.

"So how do we fix it?" I said out of nowhere.

Everyone stopped their chatter, the music on the player coming to an end at the same time.

I added, "This situation. It needs to be fixed before someone truly gets hurt." I thought of Emma trapped in The Hole, sinking deeper into insanity. "We need to get out of here."

The silence was deafening.

Then Bobby hit the end of his stick on the floor with a bang.

"We run," he said.

My eyes widened at the simplicity of the solution. But then reality smothered the dream.

"But we have nowhere to go," I added.

Brian stepped closer. "Nate and I...we have a loft next town over. It's above my family's diner. There's plenty of room for all of us. And work, too."

I turned my wide gaze to Bobby, and he nodded in response.

"It's true. We've discussed it already," he said, glancing at his friends. "Look, I'll die in here. They think I'm a cold-blooded killer. And Emma, she'll die here too if I don't get her out. She needs to be free." His eyes misted at the mention of her name, and my chest tightened. Every syllable wrapped up his deep feelings for her.

"We can do it tonight," Bobby stated. "But I won't leave without her."

His friends nodded like they were ready for the challenge.

"You won't be able to get to her," Kaitlin interjected.

I gasped at her unfiltered words as Bobby launched over to her.

"What do you mean?" he barked. "Why not?"

She faltered, looking to me for backup.

"She's in The Hole," I said. My final bits of air trailed out of me, and my eyes flickered shut.

"What the fuck is The Hole?" he blasted.

My fists tightened as I came up with the words to describe it, knowing there was no way to make it sound any less evil.

"It's solitary. In a dark cellar. Locked door...." I paused, then added, "Restraints."

"Jesus Christ!" His hands ran through his hair.

"What the fuck?" Brian exclaimed. "Is that shit for real?"

I nodded. "It's how they punish us...for the slightest offenses. To keep us subdued."

"Where is it?" Bobby stormed toward the door. "You have to show me where it is."

Terror filled my soul at the thought of bringing Bobby into the Excited Ward, especially in a rage. But it was obvious I had no choice. He would be going with or without me.

CHAPTER 15

W e raced through the dark tunnels with Bobby in the lead. Kaitlin and I followed closely behind him, and his friends kept up at the rear. The white pipes in the ceiling led us straight to the Excited Ward, and Bobby smashed his body through the door.

"Wait," I commanded. "You won't find her without us. It's a hidden alcove at the front of the building."

"Show me the goddam way," he demanded.

I stepped into the corridor of the basement, glancing over my shoulder at Brian and Nate.

"They can't come in here," I said to Bobby. Leaning into the darkness of the tunnel where they stood and repeated myself. "You can't come in. If they find you, they'll arrest you for trespassing. Or worse."

"It doesn't matter. We're here to help," Brian shot back.

"No," Bobby insisted. "I need you to stay hidden. As my secret weapons." He moved closer to the door to the tunnel where his friends remained out of view. "If anything goes wrong, I need you to take care of the girls. Got it?"

Brian frowned at his orders but accepted them, knowing Bobby needed him as backup.

"Got it," he said, retreating into the darkness with Nate. "Grace," he called. "If anything goes wrong, we'll come back for you when the dust settles. We'll find you."

I nodded and closed the door, sealing them in the tunnels. They had no idea the forces they were coming up against. The ward refused to lose, and it would never give up its charges that easily.

"Which way?" Bobby shouted with impatience.

Adrenaline pumped through me as I realized we'd gotten ourselves into a thick mess. But there was no stopping the runaway train now. Bobby was in a frenzied state. No one could stop him until he found Emma.

"Follow me," I said, and we raced through the sleeping ward toward the hidden alcove. "It's there." I pointed to the door hidden in the shadows.

Bobby pushed past me to hurl the door open.

"Emma," he shouted as he flew down the stairs.

Kaitlin and I followed, terrified his shouts would bring the wardens running.

"Bobby?" Emma's weakened voice squeaked through the door.

He ran toward the sound, then placed his ear on the second door. "Emma," he called.

"Bobby," she cried. "It's not safe. Get out of here!" Her voice cracked with sobs.

He pulled on the handle of the door, throwing his shoulder into it with all his weight. Then he stepped back and pressed against the wall across from it. With a huge hurl, he threw himself toward the door. And with a thunderous kick, he burst through it.

The crack of the wood and the smash of the force on the door sent echoing vibrations through the cellar and up into the rafters. My heart stopped, knowing they'd catch us. But, somehow, I couldn't pull myself away from the unfolding carnage.

I ran to the door. A gasp escaped my throat as I watched Bobby's horror at the sight of Emma strapped to the bed.

He dove at her, clasping her face in his hands.

"Jesus. How could they do this?" he sobbed.

He kissed her lips, then hurried to her restraints. He fumbled with the buckles undoing her arms first. As soon as he loosened the straps, she reached for him and pulled him into her.

They kissed with a burning passion I'd never seen before. Tears filled my eyes, and I prayed they would be able to find peace together.

"We need to hide." Kaitlin pulled on my arm. "If they find us here…"

Pounding footsteps and voices from the hallway above filled the space around us.

"They're coming," I called to Bobby and Emma.

"Get out of here," he yelled. "Hide! There's nothing you can do now. But you need to be able to help Emma later, so hide! Now!"

He fumbled more with her ankle straps, then Kaitlin pulled me into the suitcase room. In the same second she clicked the door shut, footsteps boomed down the stairs, followed by male shouts.

In a skirmish of thrown bodies, kicking, and wrestling, I pictured the brawny male guards from Ward B subduing Bobby.

"Look at her," Bobby screamed. "Don't you see what they are doing to her in here?" He struggled against their hold. "Help me get her out! Dear God, how can you live with yourselves?" he pleaded.

"Hold him still!" The evil voice made me lurch for the door.

Kaitlin grabbed hold of my arms to stop me from revealing our hiding spot.

"Still!" Nurse Totten's voice poisoned my mind with terror. "There now. That should calm him into a sleepy puppy. You'll have no trouble now getting him back to your high-security ward." Her tone cut at their incompetence.

They bounced and banged carrying their load all the way up the stairs. There was no telling what they would do with Bobby now.

Then Totten's voice snaked its way to our ears as she entered Emma's room.

"Now I hope your friends had nothing to do with this," she seethed. "But it doesn't matter. They'll be seeing Dr. Kilbride this morning for their examination. I'll be sure to enlighten him of their defiance." She chuckled. "But you…I'll be sure to let him know of your filth. Sending your scent across to the men's wards. Filthy whore. Have you any idea of the troubles you've brought on that boy?"

Kaitlin pulled on my frozen body, ushering me out of the suitcase room and up the stairs. Emma's sobs stabbed at my soul, weighing down each and every step.

"We're dead if she catches us," Kaitlin whispered.

I stumbled along as we crept out of the cellar into the dark alcove. But this time, my focus shifted away from racing to the safety of our rooms. It moved to what our next step toward salvation would be.

My eyes darted toward the intricately carved moldings of the foyer area, landing on the stately entryway to the ward. Oriental carpets and fancy painted vases decorated the door, giving a false sense of welcome and refinement.

I nodded at Kaitlin.

"It's now or never," I said, pointing to the front door. "I'm going that way."

~

Without hesitation, Kaitlin followed me into the foyer toward the front entryway of the Excited Ward. The darkness of the foyer assured me the door was locked tight. First, to keep any strangers out, but, more certainly, to keep all of us in.

I twisted the doorknob, shaking it, then jumped back in surprise as it cracked open.

"Oh my God," I shot at Kaitlin. "The men must have taken him out this way."

I couldn't believe it. In all the chaos, someone had left the door unlocked. But in the following second, more voices and clomping shoes filled the depths of the corridors behind the foyer. More night staff were coming to assist Nurse Totten.

I pulled the door fully open, and we raced outside. Jumping off the concrete steps onto the walkway, I ran out to the road. With every remaining ounce of energy in our bodies, we tore along the road past the chapel.

We continued beyond the mysterious Research Building, heading straight to the main entrance. Dr. Johnson hadn't parked his fancy car out front yet, but I pounded on the door anyway, in hopes an orderly or night staffer might open it.

Dawn had barely broken, and I realized the building was likely empty until the workday began. But it was Sunday, and I couldn't remember if Administration was in operation on the weekends.

I glanced back at the Excited Ward in fear that a bunch of orderlies would be tearing across the road to catch us. With no one yet in sight, I turned my attention to the chapel.

"We need to hide," I whispered to Kaitlin, out of breath. "In the chapel."

"They'll look for us in there," she whined. But her legs moved quickly as we barreled toward it.

"We just need a few hours," I panted. "Just enough time for Dr. Johnson to arrive. We have to tell him everything. He's a good man. I know he'll listen."

I pulled on the large double doors of the chapel, and they groaned open.

"Thank you, Jesus," Kaitlin cried as the doors opened and we entered the sacred space.

I closed the doors behind us, searching for a place to hide. We moved toward the altar, and I looked for a sheltered space under it.

"Maybe in there?" Kaitlin pointed to a door behind the altar area.

We entered the small room and I noticed a few religious garments hanging from hooks as well as some dinged metal chalices. I walked around, searching for a spot that would hide us both, but there just wasn't enough furniture or even a closet. I slumped against the wall and peeked over my shoulder out the window. My movement caused the wall behind me to rattle and I jumped away for a better look. There, camouflaged within the wallboards, was small door, painted the same ivory color as the walls.

I opened the hidden door, expecting a cramped storage space filled with religious trinkets, but instead, it led to a spiral staircase that ran higher than I could see.

"It's the stairs up to the clock tower," I exclaimed. "Get in here." I waved for Kaitlin to follow me.

As she squeezed in, I reached back into the room and grabbed the rim of a nearby metal trash bucket. I pulled it as close to the door as possible, just as I closed it behind us. It would hopefully hide the fact the door even existed.

In a whirl, we flew up the circling staircase, straight to the top. Internal clock mechanisms covered all four interior walls at the narrow pinnacle. A ledge traversed around the edges likely to allow for repairmen to run maintenance on the clock. We perched on the boards, gazing out across the asylum grounds from the ventilation grates below each clock face.

Dawn had broken, and rays of early morning sun glowed against the walls of the red brick buildings. A calm serenity hung over the institution, allowing a moment for us to catch our breaths.

Then all hell broke loose.

The front door of the Excited Ward smashed open as Nurse Totten and several other staff members poured out. Each traveled in a different direction—some headed around back, while others moved with agency toward the dining and rec halls.

Nurse Totten remained standing at the top of the stairs, overseeing the search efforts with her hands on her hips. My heart pounded out of my chest as her gaze moved up the clock tower and landed directly on me. She squinted as if focusing onto my soul and I deflated under her judging scrutiny. My stomach twisted in panic at being caught, but when her eyes moved away without a flinch, I realized she was only checking the time.

As the search spread out further, Totten turned and disappeared into the ward. She likely had her own ideas of locations to search for us, including the tunnels. I wondered how much she knew about them and if she had any idea about Dr. Kilbride's sinister use of the space. It wouldn't surprise me if she turned a blind eye to his deviance. She actually relied on it to help her carry out her own unjust sanctions, like the evaluations we were almost about to endure. Sickness churned in my stomach as I considered what might have become of us if we hadn't run. But then, I also had to consider what might happen since we *did* run.

I pictured Totten moving through the ward, searching all the places we could have been hiding. She'd likely be searching for a very long time.

And then a smash from below stopped our breathing. Someone had entered the chapel.

"Hello?" a voice called through the echoing structure.

Footsteps clomped across the floor and bounced through the wooden beams up to where we hid, as we remained perfectly still.

The voice moved closer, as if the person had poked their head right into the small room behind the altar. "Hello?"

High-pitched ringing in my ears replaced the sound of the orderly's voice as panic overtook me. But soon after, the sound of a closing door brought silence back to the chapel and we both exhaled in relief.

"Don't make a sound," I whispered. "He could be tricking us."

Kaitlin nodded and we remained perfectly still, watching the outside activity below.

A few staff members had regrouped at the stairs of the Excited Ward after searching the grounds behind it. But a couple of the orderlies were still unaccounted for.

The brightness of morning awakened the wards, as staff opened windows allowing unsettled, disturbed voices from the Untidy Ward to travel through the trees. The dining hall employees arrived from their quarters at the outer edge of the grounds, ready to begin the process of breakfast.

After a solid chunk of time had passed, we watched the gray sea of girls file out of the Excited Ward and enter the dining hall. I noticed Betty walking with Jeannie, while cautiously scanning the area.

"It must be eight," I whispered.

"How much longer do we have to wait here?" Kaitlin asked, fidgeting on her board.

"Until Dr. Johnson arrives," I snapped. "Maybe until tomorrow."

"What!"

"Shh." I lifted my finger to my mouth, cocking an ear to hear. "Do you have a better idea?"

My annoyed tone cut through the air, hitting Kaitlin between the eyes. She turned to stare out the air vent on the opposite side of the tower.

"Shit!" She jumped on her board, making it rattle on its brackets.

I followed her gaze out the slats, bracing myself against the sight of Dr. Kilbride marching along the road. His briefcase swung along his side in rhythm with his long strides. The stern expression on his face, focused on the Excited Ward, tensed my muscles as I strained to follow his form.

"He looks like he's on a mission," I murmured. "And with us not there, he'll aim all that negative energy at Emma. We don't have much time now."

I swung my gaze toward the Administration Building. Still no activity.

Another hour or two felt like eternity and I'd picked my cuticles raw. We slouched on our boards, twisting to relieve our backaches as well as return the blood flow to our legs.

Then, a low rumble caught my attention. I leaned in the direction of the sound, pressing my eyes against the slats of the vent and straining for a better view. As the rumble grew louder, the sound of tires on gravel sent my heart pounding.

Dr. Johnson's fine automobile rolled into view, parking outside Administration. I nearly jumped out of my skin as I scrambled onto the spiral staircase.

"Come on," I hissed. "We need to get to him before he goes inside!"

We flew down the stairs, then pushed out the small door. At full speed, we ran from the room into the altar area, then shot straight for the large double doors to the outside. And just as I prepared to sprint toward Dr. Johnson, a strong hand grabbed my elbow and pulled me back into the chapel.

CHAPTER 16

S et off-balance, I fell backward into the pews, tugging my arm from the firm grip. Kaitlin wriggled in his grasp as well, held by his other strong hand.

"Gotcha," he said. His white uniform and black belt filled my eyes with shock. I studied his face, certain I'd never seen him before—likely Patrick's replacement, fresh and eager to impress the wardens. "I knew if I waited long enough…"

I yanked my arm from his hold, then shoved him with my full body weight.

"Dr. Johnson," I screamed as I ran for the double doors. "Dr. Johnson, please!"

Footsteps sounded on the landing, and I sucked a breath in. Had he heard my cries? I stared at the doors as the shadow of a man filled the entryway.

"Give me a hand," the orderly holding Kaitlin shouted.

The man stepped farther into the chapel, revealing his own white uniform and black belt. He grabbed my arms, then yanked them behind my back, restraining me with enough force it felt as if my shoulders would dislocate.

I threw my head back in pain, cracking my skull against his lip.

"Bitch," he spat. "You split my lip!" He gripped me harder, and I winced from the pain in my muscles.

The two orderlies dragged us out of the chapel along the road toward our ward. I stared at Dr. Johnson's automobile, but he was nowhere in sight.

"Dr. Johnson," I screamed. "Please!"

He pulled my arms harder behind me. "Shut the hell up," the orderly said. "Wait until the head nurse sees this. Her purple spot will light up like fireworks."

The other orderly laughed. "She'll treat us nicer after this, I bet."

They spoke as if we weren't even there, like hunters bringing home the quarry. Then they shoved us up the stairs of the ward and into the foyer.

"We got 'em," one shouted.

Within seconds, Nurse Totten was upon us. Her grin ran up the sides of her face, nearly touching her squinting eyes.

"Well done, lads," she snapped. "Take them to the tubs. They need a good soak."

My eyes shot to Kaitlin's. Water therapy. Totten had nearly killed Emma with it—and probably caused her some level of brain damage from lack of oxygen. Kaitlin and I already suffered from brain injuries, and I was sure additional trauma would only worsen our symptoms.

"Where's Emma?" I barked.

Nurse Totten lifted her eyebrows as if affronted. She snickered. "Oh, Dr. Kilbride has taken **good** care of her. He ordered a specific treatment plan." She followed as the orderlies pushed us down the hall. "Wasn't the best idea for her to strike him. You see, now she's considered dangerous. A threat to others. We can't have that now, can we?"

My eyes widened in panic. What could she be eluding to? Her sinister tone left only the worst possibility in my mind.

"Where is she?" I shouted.

"Mind your tone, girl. Or I might have to add additional comments to your file. Ones that would land you in the same position as your friend." Her heels clomped along the tile flooring, each bang piercing through my brain. "She'll be moved to the research labs shortly."

Jesus, no! They tortured patients in there, performing barbaric operations without the person's consent. Anyone who went into that dark building always came out as a shell of their former selves. Gone forever.

Tears poured down my cheeks as I pictured them restraining her, then sending sharp pokers through her eye sockets into her brain. Their experiments with lobotomies were violent, leaving the patients drooling and babbling in the Quiet Ward.

We had to stop them.

The orderlies shoved us into the hydrotherapy room, then stood at attention like soldiers waiting for their next orders.

"Do you vow to never speak of what happens in this room? Your oath as respected staff of this facility requires confidentiality." She waited for the men to answer.

"Yes, ma'am," they said in unison.

I stared at the filled tubs and the wooden cages leaning against them. Straps hung from all sides with the metal buckles settled on the floor. Someone had prepped the room, as if awaiting our arrival. Shivers ran through my body, causing me to flinch and shudder. I looked at Kaitlin, but instantly regretted it. Tears fell from her eyes as she stared into oblivion, accepting her traumatic fate.

But I refused it.

My visions from solitary meant something. I'd seen so much of what was to come. Emma. Bobby. Their tragedies. I had to stop it.

Then Totten's voice broke through my thoughts.

"Strip them," she commanded the orderlies. "Restrain them in the tubs."

The words shot me in the heart, and I stumbled. I shook my head, a new strength raging through me, like a threatened animal had been released within me. I launched for the mop behind the tubs, grabbed it, and brandished it like a spear. At first, the orderlies and Totten recoiled. In that second of surprise, I turned and smashed the window with it.

"Dr. Johnson," I screamed. "Dr. Johns—" A hard tackle from behind made me hit the floor hard.

But that didn't stop me. "Help us, please, Dr. Johnson!"

A hand covered my mouth and nose with heavy pressure. I struggled for air, kicking my knee up with a jolt. It landed right between his legs, and he rolled off me with a sickening grunt.

"Help! Dr. Johnson," Kaitlin screamed.

Nurse Totten and the orderlies scrambled to control us, but we continued to holler at the tops of our lungs.

But then a deep kick to my ribs knocked the wind out of me. I sucked in short gulps of air, trying to regain control of my breathing. Kaitlin squirmed under the weight of the other orderly. In swift movements, they dropped us into the tubs.

I wheezed harder, fighting to breathe again as Totten tugged my arms and legs to restrain them with straps. Kaitlin struggled against the two orderlies who pressed her deeper into the water. Before her face went under, she let out one more scream.

"Dr. Johnson!"

And then silence.

Just as I regained a full breath of air, an orderly shoved my head under. My eyes shot open under the water, and I watched as the wooden cage settled over the top of the tub, keeping me below the surface. Totten's face hovered over it, distorted by the moving water, but her sinister grin was still clear as day. The burning in my lungs grew worse as the seconds ticked away, stealing pieces of my life with them.

A pounding in my head throbbed with intense pain, as my injured brain struggled to get its valuable oxygen. As unconsciousness threatened through my fading vision, new images awoke within my suppressed memories. More flashes of Emma and Bobby, but this time they were on the outside. We all were. But something was off. Something was out of place. Like we were all caught in a time warp, one that spanned dimensions beyond our grasp. I called to them, knowing they were out of place, but having no clue how to help them.

And then, with a shocking splash, my lucid thoughts and awareness of time and place resurfaced as the wooden cage flew off my tub. I launched my head up out of the water and expanded my lungs to their fullest. The sound of my huge inhale, blending with Kaitlin's similar gasp, filled the room with its harrowing resonation. We pulled in life-saving air, preparing for our second dunk, when a new voice broke into our consciousness.

A man's voice filled the room with new commands, sending another layer of terror through me until his words broke through to my mind.

"Release them at once," he boomed.

I blinked to clear the water from my eyes, straining to focus on the man by Kaitlin's tub. Then movement at my side turned my head. Another man held the wood cage over me, gaping at me with a horrified expression.

"Patrick?" I whispered, then coughed.

"You're safe now, Grace," he said gently while releasing my restraints. "I've told him everything. He's a good man. He's going to help you."

I leaned over the edge of my tub for a better look at the other man. He helped Kaitlin out of her tub before wrapping her in a dry blanket. His kind, familiar face warmed me with relief, and I knew in an instant it was Dr. Johnson.

"You've no business barging in on our rehabilitation practices," Nurse Totten's barked, her harsh voice shattering the room. "Your place is in the office. Let me tend to my role as you tend to yers." She glared at Dr. Johnson with a look that could kill.

But he didn't back down to her intimidation. Instead, he snapped right back.

"You've crossed a line, Nurse. Too much time in the madhouse, perhaps?" he taunted. "You'll be disciplined for your cruel and abusive actions."

She clomped her heels together, standing ramrod straight. "How dare you talk to me that way? Have you no idea who…"

"You," he interrupted. "You have no idea who you've crossed. I am the superintendent of this facility, and my only goal is the safety and heathy rehabilitation of these patients. To assist them in a successful transition back to productive lives." He stepped into her personal space, speaking straight into her face. "You are a misguided tyrant. You have damaged the name of this good facility. I will have you removed immediately, then have your license revoked."

Her eyes shot wide as she gasped. "We'll see about that," she grumbled, whirling before stomping down the hall, out of sight.

Dr. Johnson motioned to the two orderlies. "Gather dry clothes for these girls. And be prepared for sanctions against your inappropriate conduct."

Grumbling, they left the room to find dry frocks.

"What about Emma?" I interjected. "They're sending her to the lab for treatment. Please, we need to find her!"

I bolted for the door in my wet frock, and the others followed. As I turned out of the room, I bumped into a nursemaid standing just out of view. It was the new young one who'd been hovering just at the peripheral for the past few days.

"Oh," I gasped as I slammed into her. "Pardon me."

She stepped out of my way in silence, then glanced at Dr. Johnson with a nod.

"Where's Emma?" Dr. Johnson asked.

"They've put her in the holding room, awaiting transfer to the Research Hall," she reported.

"Show us the way," he demanded.

We followed the nurse through the winding corridors and up a flight of stairs. She slowed as she passed a nurse's station, then approached a heavy white door. It was slightly ajar, and she pulled it open in surprise.

"She's gone!"

A thin metal wire hung from the lock on the inside of the door, and I smiled at Emma's clever escape. But then images of her hanging from the tree flooded into my mind.

"She swore she'd never let them do it," I shouted.

"Do what?" Dr. Johnson stepped closer.

"A lobotomy," I yelled. "She said she'd rather die by her own doing. She refused to allow them the satisfaction."

I grabbed Kaitlin's arm. "The tree," I gasped.

Kaitlin bared her teeth as she nodded. "Yes. I've seen it, too. The hanging tree."

We tore down the hall, running at a panicked pace, praying we weren't too late. Barreling out of the front entryway of the ward, we spilled into the street, searching every tree for any sign of Emma.

The others stood panting behind us as we perused the area.

"Where would she have gone?" Patrick asked.

I closed my eyes. *Think, Grace, think.* An explosion of images flashed in my head—boarded-up buildings. Decaying structures. Signs warning of dangerous conditions. A strange automobile with a metal roof and thick black tires—almost like a space machine.

I pressed my fingers to my eyes, squeezing them tighter. Then… a flash of the tree. The one by the chapel.

A strange sound of screaming pulled my attention in the other direction before I could make a run for it. And there, in a high, barred window of Ward B, was Bobby. His frantic banging and shrill screams frightened me, but then I realized he knew what was happening as he pointed toward the chapel.

I turned and ran, faster than I ever had in my life. And just as I rounded the bend, the hanging tree came into view, its familiar low branches and heavy burdened aura, like a punch to the gut.

We raced toward it. Just as we reached its shadows, a figure fell from the branches above and swung by her neck from a rope.

A piercing scream escaped me in the same instant.

"Emma!"

CHAPTER 17

P atrick lurched forward, then grabbed onto Emma's swinging
body. He lifted her to release the tension on her neck.

Her eyes opened in surprise at the unexpected contact, and she
grabbed onto his hair and pulled.

"Ach," he cried. "Stop it. I'm saving you."

Her lips moved as she tried to speak, but only raspy hacks came
out as she continued to pull and kick.

"Emma, stop," I called. "We're here. You're safe now."

Her wild eyes met mine, at first with sharp anger for interfering
with her plan, but then they brightened.

I sprinted to her and loosened the noose around her neck. With
Patrick's help, I slid her out of it. He laid her onto the ground, leaning
against the trunk.

She reached her hand around her neck and rubbed at the burns,
which grew redder by the minute.

"Your neck will be sore for a while," Dr. Johnson said as he examined her. "But fortunately, you swung more than dropped, so you
prevented a snapped neck. A moment or two more of the swinging,
though, and you'd have asphyxiated yourself."

Kaitlin and I knelt on either side of her and I reached around her shoulders to squeeze her.

"Thank God we got here in time," I whispered. "Bobby directed us toward you. He knew. Somehow."

"Yeah," she croaked through a sore throat. "We had a pact."

"What kind of pact?" I asked, glancing back in the direction of Ward B.

"You know, the suicide kind." She grinned. "We don't want to live if we can't be together."

I pulled back in surprise, but then my shoulders relaxed. It wasn't really that surprising. Their raw love could be felt in the electric charge between them.

She continued, "And I'd be damned if I was gonna let him see me as a drooling imbecile after their barbaric treatment procedures. Not on your life."

Images of Bobby frantically calling to us returned to me, and I leapt to my feet. "I need to signal him you're okay," I called as I ran around the bend.

A light in Bobby's window pulled my eyes to it. He stood staring out, soaked as if a bucket had been spilled over his head. But then it became clear. He held a blue and white labeled can in one hand. There was no doubt it was the gas fluid for refilling his lighter. And in his other hand, the cigarette lighter glowed, scratched to life in full flame.

My hands flew up wildly to stop him. He gazed back in a lost glare that proved he believed Emma was dead. Subtle shakes of his head showed me his disappointment in the corrupted system that got them to this point. But then a smile of satisfaction lifted at the edges of his mouth as he brought the flame closer to his body.

I screamed with every ounce of my energy and flapped my arms across the front of me to signal him to stop. I shot two thumbs-up and then made okay signs with my thumbs and forefingers. He hesitated and pressed closer to his window. I smiled at him and in a near moment of disbelief, he snapped the lighter shut, extinguishing the flame.

∾

As I rounded the corner, heading back to Emma's tree, I stopped short as I stared at her on the ground with Kaitlin by her side. My body refused to move as I continued to watch the scene unfold. I'd seen it before, somehow. More than déjà vu though. Only, I couldn't shake the disturbing image of Emma's lifeless body hanging from the tree. My mind kept playing tricks on me, showing her purple face twisting at the end of the rope. But every time I blinked to clear it, she was there on the ground again, smiling over at me.

A chill shot through my body as I shook my head to clear it. I turned away, following the sound of hooves, and saw a police cart drawn by two massive horses rolled along the road by the chapel. Two officers hopped off, then straightened their derby caps. The visors hung low over their eyes, making it difficult to see their expressions. Whistles hung from chains on their lapels, shiny badges catching the sunlight. They walked in synchronized strides to us.

"Heard you called for police support, Doctor?" the first officer said.

"Yes, thank you, Constable," Dr. Johnson replied.

My heart sank as I envisioned them arresting us. Prison would be no better—it could possibly be worse. And with Emma, there was no telling what would become of her if they stripped her away from Bobby.

Dr. Johnson continued, "In the Excited Ward. Third floor. You'll find Dr. Kilbride in his office. He assaulted this woman." He pointed to Emma. "And countless others." His eyes fell in shame.

"Yes, sir," the officer said with a nod.

"And there's another," Dr. Johnson added. "Rosemary Totten. For unethical, excessive use of force and violent crimes against the patients in her care."

The officer nodded again and signaled for his partner to follow him.

"They won't be harming you ever again," Dr. Johnson spoke to Emma, then looked at Kaitlin and me. "Any of you." He exhaled as his eyes grew heavy. "I've turned a blind eye, and I am ashamed of what I've missed. I vow to you that I will correct it. I promise you."

I stared into his eyes, straight to his soul. Belief in him swelled.

"How did you know?" I asked.

Dr. Johnson looked at Patrick, then at the new nurse. "Mr. McCarthy, Patrick here, came to me the other day in secret, just after being dismissed, I believe. His report of what he'd witnessed in the ward was, shall we say, disturbing."

I looked at Patrick with wide eyes. He'd saved us. I knew he would. My heart swelled thinking of his bravery and his integrity.

"Thank you," I whispered to him. "Mr. McCarthy." And I grinned.

He smiled and dropped his eyes to the ground.

"Patrick told me of the abuse in the Excited Ward. Mistreatment, to say the least. I then placed Mary in the ward." He glanced at the young nurse and nodded. "She was my mole. A spy, you could say. And she confirmed everything he had reported." His eyes fell. "And more."

We were speechless. The three of us stared at each other, then at Patrick and Mary.

"Thank you," I said to all of them. "For saving us."

They nodded, but the look of sorrow in their eyes proved they felt it wasn't enough. Or maybe that it was too late, the extent of the damage too deep.

"I'll have you girls stay in the TB House now," Dr. Johnson said. "It's been cleared of the tuberculosis bacteria for over a decade now. It will be safe and comfortable. Mary will be your nurse there." He paused. "I doubt you'll want to step foot back in your own ward. Not until all is settled, anyway."

I nodded my head in agreement. I never wanted to set foot in the Exited Ward ever again. Its walls held too much power over me, suffocating me.

I considered the idea of the TB House. Last time I walked past it, I pretended it was my own sweet cottage. Hidden behind the Quiet Ward, it looked like a place Hansel and Gretel might find in the woods. It was the closest thing to a home anywhere within the borders of the heartless institution.

Then Patrick moved a little closer and leaned down toward my ear. "Maybe I'll see you someday. You know, on the outside."

I lifted my eyes to meet his. "I'd like that."

He stood taller and stepped back, trying to remain aloof, but he kept his eyes on me and their twinkle made me smile. Emma fidgeted as she watched us.

"What about Bobby?" she interjected, jumping back to her own predicament. "They took him away. He's being punished for trying to help me."

Dr. Johnson turned to her. "I didn't realize that. I'll have a look into it right away," he assured her. "Bobby's one of my patients, for therapy. A fine young man with promise. I'll be certain he's treated properly."

Emma smiled, exhaling loudly. She looked at me with relief as the weight of her worry lifted.

"I wish you girls had some place to go. Something to aspire to," he added. "I can see that without hope or a dream, one could get lost in here." He hesitated in thought. "I'll work better rehabilitation into the plan for the institution. To teach you skills for the outside world and to encourage interaction with the local townsfolk."

His ideas sounded hopeful. And modern. For the first time in a long time, it felt like there could be an end to this madness.

But I couldn't wait that long. I was ready to get out of here *now*.

I'd found my spirit, and she was strong. I'd go crazy if I spent any more of my life within this confining prison.

I caught Kaitlin's eyes, and she shone the same resolve back at me. She was ready to go, too.

I turned to Emma. She dropped her eyes from mine and turned away, for she was not.

We wasted no time moving into the TB House. Under the close watch of Nurse Mary—and the expectation to join in all activities with the other patients—we still felt like prisoners. Our freedom still wasn't ours.

The cottage was homey and felt safe though, except for the random thought of tuberculosis creeping out of the plaster walls. I shuddered at the idea of the patients who'd been sent here at the height of the TB epidemic—sent here to die alone.

After just a few days in the halfway house, as Dr. Johnson called it, my head had cleared and my thoughts raced with specific plans of leaving.

"There's something I need to get from the ward," Kaitlin said as we made our beds.

"Are you kidding me? I'm not ready to step foot back in that place yet." A chill shook my shoulders.

"I'll go." Emma's head popped up.

"Figures," I mumbled.

For her, it was like none of it ever happened. Emma rolled with the chaos—even actually seemed to crave it.

"I plan to get back in those tunnels before long, if you know what I mean," she said with a giggle.

I shook my head at her one-track mind. I still couldn't get my head around the fact that she wanted to stay here longer. Maybe I'd chosen to ignore it all this time, maybe she belonged here. But no matter how I tried, I couldn't believe that. Her anti-social, anti-establishment tendencies could find a place to survive out there somewhere. But it was Bobby. His hold on her was equally as strong as the power of the ward. Her lure to this place was compounded by both.

I shifted my attention back to Kaitlin. "What do you need from the ward?"

We didn't have any personal belongings, and I couldn't think of anything else she might want.

"It's something I saw." She hesitated. "In the cellar."

"What?" I blurted. "You want to go back to The Hole?"

"No! Of course not," she shot back. "The suitcase room."

My intrigue rose to the ceiling. What could she have seen in the suitcase room that was worthy of going back to that hellhole? But my apprehension shut down my curiosity.

"I don't know," I murmured, fearing the pull of the ward. "What if we get trapped in there somehow? My dreams keep showing it. Boarded up windows, no way out. Should we really chance going back in there?"

"Don't be such a sissy," Emma teased. "That's just a bunch of hocus pocus."

Kaitlin chewed on her thumbnail. "I know what you mean. It does seem kind of risky to go back in there. Like playing with fire."

Nurse Mary turned off the gas from under the kettle, bouncing nervously. "I'll take you there," she said. "I'll make sure nothing happens to you. That no one interferes."

"Perfect!" Emma leaped toward the door. "Let's do it."

I gazed at Mary, astounded by her offer to help us with a mission she knew nothing about. Watching her helpful preparations, I realized she knew we weren't crazy. She knew we didn't belong here. And that was enough for her.

"Thank you, Mary," I said. "We really appreciate your help."

She lifted a shoulder up to her ear and walked to the door. In that moment, I saw the adventurous side of her. She was intrigued by Kaitlin's offer and in that moment, she was one of us.

The four of us walked toward the Excited Ward, and I couldn't help but glance at the hanging tree. Somehow, we were able to stop the tragedy that almost occurred that day. I felt a ripple quiver through the universe that shook my soul deeply. It settled within me as if the shift were meant to be.

Mary led us through the Excited Ward to the cellar door hidden in the darkness of the alcove. At first, I was reluctant to go down. The memories were too vivid and frightening. But then, Emma pushed past me and flew down the stairs. We followed without hesitation.

Emma shot straight for The Hole, then stood in the doorway of the torture chamber that held so much darkness for her. Her hands clamped on the sides of the entryway, her knuckles going white.

"It's to be sealed off," Mary said in a quiet tone. "Permanently."

It was the right thing to do. That space was full of evil now. For all of us.

"Good," I spat.

Although it also held parts of our souls, torn from us in strips. Best to be sealed up, though, I supposed.

"Funny how easily one forgets," Emma murmured as she stepped into the horrific space. "All I remember is the revelations. The mind-expanding illumination. I am meant to be here," she said. "Meant to…stay."

"What? No, you're not!"

"No, really. I am." She turned to us. "I figured it all out while locked in the darkness. I'm here for Bobby. To heal him. Don't you see?" She stepped closer. "I'm supposed to be dead. I was meant to hang from that tree. And you know it. I can see it in your eyes, the way you look at me."

Chills ran up my spine as if she were inside my head.

"But somehow, I'm still here. I'm alive," she continued. "And I have a purpose that was revealed to me in my darkest hour." She grinned. "And it's Bobby."

My heart sank as her words seeped through my armor. She had no intention of leaving with us. Ever.

My plans of getting out of here would only include Kaitlin. The thought of leaving Emma here made my heart ache. She was one of us. Somehow, she was what awakened me, what brought me back to awareness of myself. It was as if she called to me, deep within my soul, and brought me out of hiding.

If she hadn't reached me, the true me, I wouldn't have been able to save her. It was as if it had all come full circle.

"Come on out of there," Mary interjected, waving her hand at Emma. "It's not good for you to be in there, reliving the trauma. Come."

Emma smiled at Mary with a sympathetic smirk that mocked her superficial beliefs. The glow in Emma's eye proved she'd reached a higher level of awareness than all of us combined.

Kaitlin moved toward the other door. "Come on. You guys have to see this."

I followed her, but I made sure Emma was coming as well. She was reluctant to leave The Hole at first, like it held some creepy nostalgia for her, but finally she pulled herself out of the doorway and caught up.

Kaitlin opened the door. Light from the hall filled the room, casting shadows along the back wall lined with stacked suitcases.

"A storage room?" Emma asked impatiently.

"Better." Kaitlin pulled one of the cases out of the pile, then placed it in front of us. She flicked the tag into view to reveal the writing on it. *Kaitlin Edwards*

"My belongings," she said with wide eyes. "All of our belongings." Kaitlin pointed to the other cases. Immediately, Emma and I found our own tucked in near the spot where hers had been.

I pulled my suitcase out of the hoard, holding it to my chest like I'd found a long-lost piece of myself.

"Oh my God, Kaitlin," I said on an exhale. "Thank you."

Emma wiggled on the buckles of her suitcase, ready to pop it open.

"Wait," Kaitlin said. "We need to do this carefully. Like, we don't know what we'll find or how it will be."

She was right. Anything could be in our suitcases. Evidence of our former lives before the ward. Maybe we'd remember or maybe not. But we needed to proceed with caution.

"Let's bring them back to the house and open them there," I said.

Emma stepped toward another random case sitting apart from the rest. She flipped the lid open and peered in. "The coat!" She beamed. She pulled the peacoat out of the case and gave it a shake. "This coat saved my life. Well, you did, Grace."

I reached for the garment and stroked its woolen sleeve, knowing how much it helped Emma that night. I was sure it belonged to Betty and I could easily envision her wearing it. I hoped one day it would be returned to her.

Then Emma tore out of the room with the coat. She stood at the entrance to The Hole and gazed in. Before I could stop her, she entered the dark space. I watched her place the peacoat on the metal slab where she'd been held. She systematically laid it out and secured it to the table with the restraints that hung from the sides.

"There," she said. "So no one will ever be cold here again."

CHAPTER 18

W e lined the suitcases in a row on the floor of the sitting room at the TB House. Crouching on our knees, each in front of our own cases, we stared at the mysteries that hid within.

"Who first?" Mary said.

"Kaitlin," I said. "You found them. You should go first."

Smiling, she reached for her suitcase. The faded plaid exterior had two lines of metal straps that ran around it. The buckles reminded me of our restraints, and my stomach twisted. My heart raced, heating up my face, and a strong urge to run overtook me. Closing my eyes, I focused on my breathing. I supposed I'd never be rid of the haunting trauma when even simple things like a belt buckle could trigger reliving it.

Kaitlin loosened the straps, and I refocused on her. As the buckles fell to the floor, she flipped open the small fasteners at the seal and it popped open. Kaitlin took a short breath before lifting the lid all the way up.

We leaned in with wide eyes, staring at her clothing and feminine accessories. A framed picture of a handsome couple lay on top, and she pulled it in close to her heart. Tears fell from her eyes as she reached back into the case. Moving the clothing to the side, she lifted out a perfume bottle with a pump hanging off the side and attempted to spray it at her neck. Then a notebook with a pencil sticking out from the binding.

"Do you recognize everything?" I asked impatiently.

She hesitated. "Not really. Just like, feelings. Lots of feelings."

She dug a little further, pushing a heavy skirt and thick shawl to the side. Snagging a lighter piece of fabric, she gave it a shake. The shirt looked like a garment a soldier would wear under his uniform or maybe something a laborer would wear in the mines.

"What is it?" I asked.

She turned the short-sleeved shirt so we could see the front. It had strange markings on it, like paint. Fancy scrawl ran across the middle, faded and chipping.

"Nir-nirvana?" I sounded out the letters. "What's that?"

"It's my favorite shirt," Kaitlin murmured in a confused tone. One eye narrowed as she studied it. "I don't remember it, really. But it's my favorite. I just know it."

"I've never seen anything like it before," I stated, reaching to touch the soft fabric. "But I can picture it on you, like it was something you wore all the time."

A strange sensation tickled my fingers as I touched it. My memory was triggered somehow and I was sure I heard music and felt wind blowing through my hair.

"Well, it looks like a piece of shit to me," Emma scoffed. "Something a sweaty man would wear. What the hell, Kaitlin? I thought you'd have more fashion sense." She laughed.

Kaitlin pulled her frock over her head, then tugged the shirt on. Grinning, she wrapped her arms around herself. She reached into the case, pulled out the long skirt, and then stepped into it.

Suddenly, she looked like a girl from the outside—someone who had a life, a purpose.

"You look, I don't know, normal," I said.

"Open yours," Kaitlin pressed.

Taking a deep breath, I reached for mine. The black exterior was scratched and worn, with cracked brown leather straps. I unfastened them with shaking hands, then opened the lid.

My breath sucked in as I stared at the strange contents. The plain clothing didn't even seem to be mine, and I pushed it away in disappointment. But underneath, loose objects rattled about. I rustled through, stopping to pull out a metal compact. Inside was a photo of a woman. She looked sad and lost. I snapped it shut quickly before reaching in again. My hand wrapped around the ivory handle of a hairbrush, and I immediately pulled it through my hair. Then my gaze fell on an unusual shiny glass piece. It was thin and rectangular, about the size of my hand. I balanced it in my palm, testing the weight of it.

"What's that?" Kaitlin leaned over. "It looks like a mirror, only the reflection is black."

I squinted at the glass cover, making out a light shadow of numbers deep within it.

"It's like a top-secret device they'd use in the war or something. I've never seen anything like it." I turned it over in my hand, wondering if it had actually come from outer space. "It has a picture of an apple in the center, with a bite taken out of it." Above the apple was a tiny window with two little blue lights peering out like eyes. I flipped it over quickly and studied the glass side again, squinting to read the faded numbers. "Four, dot, dot, three, zero."

The numbers flashed in my eyes as four-thirty, and I dropped the thing back into the case. I jumped to my feet, pacing as my breath accelerated beyond control.

"Hands on your knees," Mary commanded. "You're hyperventilating."

Her voice morphed through my mind as I searched for the meaning of the numbers. My entire existence hung on them. The strange device had a connection to me somehow. A deep one.

"I'm okay," I panted. "It just triggered something in me. Something big." I held my head to keep in from exploding. My brain was expanding within my skull, and I was more awake than any other time in my life. "I'm ready to get out of here," I stated.

I grabbed an outfit from the case, then changed in a matter of seconds.

"You next," I called to Emma. "Let's see what's in your case."

Emma flinched, shooting a glance at her suitcase. With a shrug, she reached for it.

Her case was dark brown and thoroughly battered. She dragged it closer, then popped open the buckles.

As she lifted the lid, her face went pale. She turned the case to expose the contents to us. And it was empty.

"It was a farce," she stated. "Your cases prove you were just passing through. Visiting, so to speak. And you would return to your lives when your stay was complete." She turned to gaze out the window. "Not me. They committed me here with no expectation I'd ever return to the outside. A one-way ticket."

My jaw fell as I stared into the empty case.

"I told you," she continued. "I was meant to be here. To stay."

I put on all the best garments from my case, then filled my jacket pockets with the trinkets. Kaitlin did the same. Whatever items we couldn't fit on our persons, we left in the cases, sealed tight to be stored as evidence of our passing through.

"Mary," Emma said in a proper tone. "Will you take me to the dining hall, please? Lunchtime is nearly here."

Mary looked puzzled at first as she glanced between Kaitlin and me. But then she nodded. "Sure, Emma. And you two? You'll meet us there?"

Her simple expression gave away no signals of what she was actually thinking, but I believed she knew exactly what we planned.

"We'll be right along," I assured her.

"Well then…" Her words stuck in her throat. "See you soon." And with a nod, she stepped out the door and waited for Emma.

Emma reached her arms around Kaitlin and me, pulling us close.

"Come visit me, will you? In the tunnels?" she whispered.

I nodded, speechless, as tears stung my eyes.

"You know," she added. "You'll do great things. You're survivors. Travelers. Ahead of your time, really. Modern thinkers." She tapped the side of head. "You're going to make a difference." She fell silent for a moment. "You already have."

"I don't want to leave you here," I whimpered.

"It's okay. I'll be fine," she said. "I can't explain it, but Bobby and I are meant to be here together. It's my destiny to be with him and I'd never choose to be anywhere else. But don't worry, we'll find our way out of here...when the time is right." She smiled and her happiness shone from her eyes. "Like I say, being crazy is a gift. One that lets me see the truth with clarity. And I see truth in all of this...and in you two."

I squeezed her harder, sobbing into her shoulder.

"Tread cautiously, though," she warned. "The ward has a powerful hold on you. One that will never truly let you go."

CHAPTER 19

As soon as Emma and Mary were out of sight, we dashed out of the TB House and ran for the woods behind it. We traveled along the edge of trees, making our way around the perimeter of the asylum grounds.

"The road that leads to the main gate is this way," I said, pointing.

As we moved past the nurse's quarters and the infirmary, the black metal gates of the entryway came into view.

"But we might be seen on the road," Kaitlin whispered. "Shouldn't we stay to the woods?"

I stopped, considering her words. It would be dangerous to go straight into the woods. We had no idea how far they went or if we'd be lost. We weren't prepared to spend a cold night in the forest. But she was right. Being seen on the road was a bigger risk we couldn't afford to take.

Just as I opened my mouth to agree, the sound of horse hooves and rickety cart wheels stole our attention. We positioned ourselves behind trees, peering toward the gates. Within moments, a cart of new patients came into view—mostly women in long skirts, each with a suitcase by their feet. All had long, worn faces. Several with splats of rotten tomatoes strewn across their clothing. As always, the towns-folk would line up every first Saturday of the month to greet the new patients—with hostility and humiliation, like a circus.

At the back of the cart, two of the men pushed to the edge. In the blink of an eye, they hopped off the cart and stole into the woods.

"That looked like Brian!" I gasped.

"It was," Kaitlin agreed. "And Nate."

I had nearly forgotten about their promise to return for us. They wouldn't let Bobby down and stuck to their plan. They had a place for us to stay and jobs while we got settled on our own. It was a miracle we caught a glimpse of them.

"They'll be heading to Ward B, I bet." I stared into the section of woods where they disappeared.

"We can't go back there now," Kaitlin whimpered. "We have to keep going."

"I know. We just have to pray Bobby or Emma get word to them that we ran." I reached into my pocket to check for the piece of paper Brian had given me when we were in the tunnels, with the address of his family's diner. "We'll have to meet them by the restaurant, I guess...once we find it."

"Let's at least try to find *them* in the woods first," she pressed.

"Okay, this way." I pushed through the overgrowth in the direction they had gone.

We shimmied through the thick brush, thorns and twigs snagging in our clothes and scratching our hands. As we pushed through a maze of moss-covered trees, uncertainty about the direction of the boys twisted us around.

"There's narrow trail over here," Kaitlin called.

We ran for it. After following it for several minutes, brightness opened ahead of us.

"I think it's a clearing." I pointed. "Like a meadow."

We picked up our pace, then burst out of the darkness of the thick woods into a rolling field of lush grass. A large mound sat on the far side, drawing our attention to its peculiar existence as it rose out of nowhere.

A knot formed in my throat, and I struggled to swallow.

"I'd heard stories about a mass grave." My voice cracked.

"You don't think that's it, do you?"

"I'm not sure." I stared at the lone hill. "It was two years ago, they said...the influenza epidemic. I heard about nine patients died every week."

We stepped further into the field, continuing to search for the boys while keeping our eyes on the mound.

Treading lightly on the soft moss, I whispered, "Let's have a closer look."

We stumbled across the bumpy field, making our way toward the mysterious mound. The faster we moved, the more we tripped and staggered across random stones buried in the ground.

"What are all these rocks?" Kaitlin huffed, steadying herself.

And just as her words came at me, my foot caught on a stone and I fell to my knees.

"Crap!" Wetness in the mossy grass soaked through the layers of my skirt, leaving mud stains.

I pulled my foot away from the square stone, leaning in for a better look.

"It's concrete," I said, pushing the long grass away from it. "And it has numbers."

Kaitlin stepped closer, then kicked the grass away from another stone. "This one, too—136." She sidestepped and found another. "148."

My eyes widened as a chill surged through my body.

"It's the cemetery," I gasped. "The patients are buried here with only numbers as their grave markers." My breath grew shallow as I struggled to get air.

"235," Kaitlin murmured with a shake in her voice.

"236," I called back.

We ran along the rows of stones, kicking the grass away to check numbers as we moved. Soon, we found the section where the stones started with the number two. The blood drained from my face as we dropped to our knees—searching for *our* numbers? *What...* My brain felt as if it would explode. It didn't make sense.

"223," Kaitlin choked.

We were getting closer.

My vision narrowed to pinprick focus on the stones in front of me. Then the sound of my name broke through my skull.

"Grace!" A girl's voice echoed through the trees, trailing off on the wind. "Kaitlin!"

Someone was calling for us. It sounded like Emma.

"Where are you?" her voice called on the wind.

My nerves spiked with terror.

"Do you hear that?" I screeched.

"Yes!" Kaitlin searched all around us. "Emma?" she called.

"Emma!" I yelled with her.

Her voice filled the cemetery. "Wait! I have something to tell you."

I searched across the cemetery toward the tree line for any sign of her and my eyes fell on the metal gate leading into the cemetery. Its familiarity haunted me to my core, and I ran to it. Stumbling and falling, I struggled to get to the gate as time morphed and slowed me like a bad dream.

"Kaitlin! Come on," I screamed.

"Grace! Kaitlin," her hoarse voice yelled to us from the woods.

I burst through the black metal gate, turning to see the front of it. A brass plaque hung from the decorative iron scrolls. I stared at it as tears of terror poured down my face.

Kaitlin caught up, pivoting to see what I was staring at. Her hands flew to her mouth as she whimpered.

Remember us, for we, too, have lived, loved, and laughed

A scream grew in my throat as my world imploded in on me. My mind shattered into a million pieces as Kaitlin's screeches shot through my soul. My vision blurred, and I covered my face with my hands. Shrieks deep within me tore up my insides as I stumbled back into the cemetery.

Gripping Kaitlin's wrist, I dragged her back to the stones and dropped to my knees. Pushing the moss and grass away, we uncovered the ones that called to us.

235...

236...

Hoarse sounds ripped out of my throat, filling the cemetery with my horror.

"Grace! Kaitlin!" The sound grew deeper as it got closer, breaking through our shredded cries. Instead of Emma's voice, it sounded like two now, the voices of two young men. It must be Brian and Nate. Maybe they'd followed Emma and were coming to get us.

I lifted my gaze, blinking to clear the fog away. The woods blurred into a smear of green and black as the sky melted into it. The only clarity in my sight was directly in front of me.

And there, hovering above us, panting from excursion, were Braden and Nick.

I knew them. So well

It was like looking upon loved ones returned from the grave—like I hadn't seen them in a hundred years.

"Grace, it's all right," Braden's voice soothed as he wrapped his arm around my shoulder.

I looked down in confusion, gaping at the stone by my knees. Next to the small square number, there was now a modern, shiny stone with words engraved in the granite.

Grace Frances Parker
1900 - 1920

But it didn't mark the date of my death, as I had originally thought.

It marked the day of my new life. The date of my escape from Blackwood Asylum.

EPILOGUE

"What happened back there?" Braden prodded. "You guys burst out of that shuttered ward like you were being chased by a ghost." He stared across the cemetery toward the grounds of the condemned state hospital. "How did you even get in there? The boards are screwed on tight."

Kaitlin and I stared speechlessly at the gravestones. Terror lingered in Kaitlin's eyes, then faded with each passing blink. Our names reached out to us from the stones, but, instead of fear, I felt a strange sense of calm.

It was like a dream, but not.

We had to help someone. And we did.

"Emma," I whispered to Kaitlin. "We saved her."

Understanding washed over Kaitlin's face.

"She reached out to us." Her hand went over her mouth. "It's like she lured us here, to get us to help her."

I nodded, processing every word. "And we did."

"But how are we back here now? Why?" She glanced up at the boys, who were pacing nervously.

"I don't know." I rubbed my head as a migraine threatened. "Do you think it's our heads playing tricks on us again? Maybe none of this is real."

"But it was real. Emma. Nurse Rotten. Dr. Johnson..." Kaitlin's voice trailed off as I jumped to my feet.

"Dr. Johnson," I yelped, sprinting for the cemetery gate.

Whipping around to the front of it, I found what I hoped would still be there. The plaque dedicated to his memory.

In dedication to Dr. Thomas Johnson
Superintendent of Blackwood Asylum 1896 - 1936
For your selfless service to these souls so they may never be
forgotten
"For we, too, have lived, loved, and laughed."

"He saved us." I turned to Kaitlin. "His compassion. And his intuition. He knew we didn't belong there."

Kaitlin's eyes narrowed as she studied my face.

"What?" She rubbed her head with a wince.

"Dr. Johnson," I repeated. "He...and Patrick." I lost track of my thoughts. "They..."

I closed my eyes and tried to remember, but everything was fading so quickly. Their faces. The girls in the ward. They all reached for me, calling my name. But it all faded beyond my sight, blowing away on the gentle breeze.

"Tom," I shouted to Braden. "Where's Tom Johnson?"

I vaguely remembered he'd been showing the boys around the research building when we'd been trapped in the ward.

"We lost him," Braden said, lifting his shoulders.

"Yeah, he just vanished," Nick added. "Ditched us."

I pinched the space between my eyes.

"What happened to us?" Kaitlin murmured.

The boys walked closer to us with gentle steps. Their worried expressions studied us for any unexpected outbursts. They'd clearly seen enough for one day.

"Let's get you two home," Braden said. "You need to rest. Doctor's orders."

"Doctor?" The word caused flashbacks to flicker in my mind.

"Yeah, you know, concussions." He placed his hand on top of my head, catching my eyes. "I'll take care of you," he whispered.

The familiar kindness in his voice soothed me deep within, and the warmth in his eyes reminded me of… what was his name? A boy who once helped me. He said we would meet again, on the outside.

Braden smiled as if seeing me clearly for the first time, as if now fully allowed. I'd let him in. And he liked it.

He reached his arm around my shoulders, guiding me toward the road. Kaitlin and Nick followed, but she and I kept glancing back to the cemetery. There was still something there. Something tremendous. I yearned to return to figure out what it was.

My eyes moved along a giant mound at the far side. In the same instant, a thousand voices cried out to me.

Gasping, I stopped short. Kaitlin halted in her tracks as well, wide-eyed with terror.

"Come on." Nick flicked his head in the direction of the car. "Legit. We need to get out of here."

They were right. We needed rest. Something enormous had just happened, and our souls were still recovering, piecing themselves back together.

I pushed my hands into the pocket of my hoodie. My fingers hit against a folded piece of paper, and I pulled it out. My eyes flicked to Kaitlin's, and she was by my side in two strides.

I unfolded the paper as we stared at it, both holding our breath.

The top of the sheet said—*Medical History.*

My air sucked in as I examined the document.

Written at the top was the name *Emma Grangley*.

My eyes moved down the form.

Prescriptives: hydrotherapy and lobotomy

I searched lower, looking for the inevitable *Deceased* stamp.

But at the bottom, there was a final section of writing I'd never seen before.

Summary: Missing. At large, dangerous. Traveling with man wanted for murder, Robert 'Bobby' Hayes.

Kaitlin and I raced back into the cemetery. We searched for the stone next to ours. 237... 237... 237... We searched for it, but we only found moss.

And then the hairs on the nape of my neck stood, sending shivers down my spine. A flash of her face and flowing blonde hair blinded me, then her words haunted my thoughts.

The ward has a powerful hold on you. One that will never truly let you go.

I covered my ears to block the insidious words from penetrating my mind. But it was too late.

Kaitlin whispered, "You heard that?"

I swallowed hard. Nodded.

"Yes." And then I glanced toward the direction of the ward. "It's still calling to us."

We glanced at our stones again, trying to remember the journey we'd just experienced. It had faded, but its memory was clamped onto our hearts.

"The cemetery," Kaitlin murmured. "It's like a passageway of some sort."

That was exactly what I'd just been thinking. Somehow, the ward had led us here and it was this place that understood our pasts. We'd had a past, many years ago, at this eerie asylum.

"It's the hold of the ward," I said. "It has a power over us, somehow. We need to get out of here and never come back."

She nodded, keeping her eyes on her stone and I held my gaze on my own as well. Then a flinch next to us drew our attention to the next stone. Our eyes fell on the elusive marker 237, now revealing itself from under the moss. Bare feet sank into the grass at the edge of the gravestone and the toes wiggled with dirt on them, having just cleared away the overgrowth. My eyes trailed up along the gray fabric of an old-fashioned dress and I froze in shock as I stared at a familiar ink stain on the pocket. Lifting my gaze higher, I peered into the face of a girl I knew.

Her long, blonde hair was disheveled, and a crazed look shot from her eyes as she gaped at us. And then, with a raspy voice, hoarse from yelling, she spoke.

"Where's Bobby?"

The End

If you are ready for Book Three, be sure to grab a copy of The Forgotten Ward.

Also, at the end of this book you will find a sample of The Forgotten Ward.

AFTERWORD

I hope you enjoyed Book Two of the Asylum Savant Series, The Excited Ward.

Be sure to visit my website for more information about this series, Book Three: The Forgotten Ward, and my other books.

Thank you!

www.jenniferrosemcmahon.com
   To sign up for my newsletter:
   https://www.subscribepage.com/f1p9w6

ACKNOWLEDGMENTS

A huge thank you to my urban explorer partner and eldest son, Rory McMahon. For your enthusiasm for this story to be told and the adventurous research that brought it to life in a way that never would have been possible without your help. Thank you, me boy, for the camaraderie, support, and love.

Thank you to Cynthia Shepp for her amazing editing super powers.

Thank you to Rebecca Frank, designer goddess, for her fabulous book covers.

And lastly, to John Thompson, Chair of the Medfield State Hospital Building and Grounds Committee, for sharing the history of the institution and providing a top-notch tour around the grounds. Many of his stories are woven into this book and brought back to life. Thank you so much for the warm welcome, and generosity of time and knowledge.

ABOUT THE AUTHOR

Jennifer Rose McMahon is a USA Today Bestselling Author and voracious urban explorer. She has been creating her Pirate Queen series, Irish Mystic Legends series, and Asylum Savants series since her college days abroad in Ireland. Her passion for Irish legends, ancient cemeteries, medieval ghost stories, and abandoned asylums has fueled her adventurous story telling, while her husband's decadent brogue carries her imagination through the centuries. When she's not in her own world writing about castles and curses, she can be found near Boston in the local coffee shop, yoga studio, or at the beach...most often answering to the name 'Mom' by her fab children four.

For more information
www.jenniferrosemcmahon.com
info@jenniferrosemcmahon.com

SAMPLE OF THE FORGOTTEN WARD, BOOK THREE

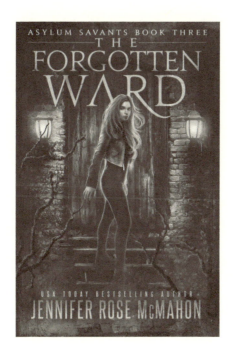

THE FORGOTTEN WARD CHAPTER 1

W ild hair and a shredded gray frock startled me at first, but it was the unhinged, crazed look in her eye that made me jump back. I stared as she tore her fingers through her matted blonde locks in desperation to make sense of her strange setting.

My disbelieving eyes fought to reject what I was seeing, but it was too late. The image had already burned onto my brain, and there was no unseeing it.

She was here.

And it wasn't right.

On the other hand, I was quick to accept the fact that Kaitlin and I had made the leap back to modern day, somehow, through the cemetery. That part had been expected, or at least, hoped for.

Confirming our current time and place, Braden and Nick hovered at the edge of the graveyard, nervously waiting for a thorough explanation of what the hell had just happened.

But now, having her here with us too, made no sense and every nerve in my body cried out in disastrous warning.

She didn't belong here.

She was from the past.

But then, so were we.

The only difference was--she was meant to stay there.

My mind twisted, folding through the complex time warp that was now my reality. I strained to be sure of where I was, back to my original, modern life.

But which one was the right one?

I'd just returned from a past existence that scared me to my core. The vile abuse and evil tyranny of the old asylum coursed sickness through my veins, tweaking my flight response with every breath.

The deranged concept of having lived a previous life in that hostile place generated a sharp pain behind my left eye. My hand flew up and smacked over it as I winced.

And then she spoke, forcing my attention back to her presence here.

"Where's Bobby?" Her eyes narrowed on me.

Her sharp tone held unnerving accusation. Suspicion.

"Emma..." My scratching voice stuck in my throat. "It's me, Grace. And Kaitlin's here." I stepped closer to help her see the details of my face. "Something strange has happened to us. I need to explain it to you."

But a clear explanation was far beyond my reach, having no idea where to start. Should I begin with the cemetery being some kind of portal to the ward's past? That she'd accidentally leaped to the future with us... without Bobby. My heart pounded in my chest by the simple mention of his name in my thoughts. She'd go insane if she believed she was separated from him, by a hundred years.

Think, Grace, think.

She stared at me, head tipped like I was stupid. "Well, I'm going back before they notice we're gone."

Emma stepped in the direction she'd initially come through the woods, but her assertive confidence soon shifted to reluctant confusion as she struggled to recognize her surroundings.

Things had changed a lot since when she first arrived here, in what felt like only moments ago. But the trees were now taller, and heavy forest overgrowth hid any clear access back to the asylum. Though, the shiny stone slab under her foot was what caught her attention most as she tripped on it.

"Ouch!" She stumbled over the edge of the stone marker and glared at it in annoyance. With a startled blink, she took a double-take as something about it caught her eye. "What the hell is that?" She bent down to inspect it closer.

I shot my eyes to Kaitlin in fear.

There was no telling how Emma would react to seeing her own gravestone, complete with death date. I recalled the surreal feeling all too well.

When I'd seen my own for the first time, I spiraled into a shock that felt like insanity. The madness went so deep, it had the power to launch me to another realm--the realm of my original existence, as an oppressed patient in the Blackwood Insane Asylum. It now stood within the clearing of the trees as a rotting ruin, boarded up and condemned.

"What the fuck?" Emma lifted her gaze to us. "They made my head-stone before I'm even dead?" She looked again at the details. "1920? What the hell? Did they plan to kill me this year or something?" She glanced at the stones beside hers and studied the ones with our names on them. "You guys, too? A conspiracy? I knew it! Those bastards plan to get rid of us."

She had no idea.

Her interpretation of the immediate facts made sense, from her current perspective, but she was so wrong.

It was now 2019, one hundred years ahead of her life, and the truth of what really occurred was about to make her lose her mind.

Kaitlin stared at me, waiting for a sound response for Emma, but only fragments of sentences and pieces of words bounced around in my mouth. I had nothing.

"Who's that?" Nick called over as he and Braden walked closer.

Emma startled. "Stay back!" Her hand flew up to stop them. "We've done nothing wrong," she shouted.

"It's okay, Emma," I said. "They're with us."

"Who the hell *are* they?" she sneered. "They look like constables-in-training or sloppy orderlies." She frowned at them in disregard.

"No, they're our friends," Kaitlin said with a nervous, half-chuckle. "They can help us."

Emma frowned.

Her reaction made sense, though. Braden and Nick looked nothing like young men she usually saw. Their hair was longer, and their clothing was more casual than the proper attire of men from the early 1900s. They probably looked comical to her.

"Where are Brian and Nate?" Emma asked, eyeballing the guys. "I thought you were going to meet up with *them*."

I closed my eyes for a moment, trying to picture Brian and Nate. I knew who they were, Bobby's friends, but I just couldn't see their faces in my mind. Everything turned to a blur so quickly and I struggled to hold the complex details of what had just happened.

But Emma was correct about them. We had planned to escape the ward and meet up. Maybe we had. Hopefully, we had. And perhaps they helped give us a fresh start to a good life.

If it was true, and we escaped the asylum for good, that would explain why we blasted back here. Possibly, by going back to our early time in the ward, we'd settled an imbalance in our pasts. One that had haunted us relentlessly and disrupted our current lives.

I thought about the past and having stopped Emma from hanging herself at the last moment, just before Bobby attempted to ignite himself with lighter fluid. Their suicide pact had nearly become a reality, one that I believed wasn't meant to be.

So, I'd interrupted fate.

And that action shifted something deep within me as if a ripple effect had moved through time, settling into my damaged soul. It left me feeling... whole, like a gaping wound had healed.

Healed. For the first time.

It felt good.

Until I looked back at Emma.

The sight of her standing here with us in the cemetery generated a deep pit in my stomach. The twist in my gut left no uncertainty that something was very wrong.

She didn't belong here with us.

I'd influenced the past, and now something was off.

She had crossed over by accident. Without Bobby.

She still had no idea what was really happening.

And it was time for me to tell her.

Before I could explain anything, Emma stormed toward the cemetery gate, brushing past Braden and Nick as if they were only in the way. Their eyes followed her, and without a word, they turned to us for an explanation. But the only answer we had was one that would blow their minds beyond the point of the wreckage they'd already experienced.

In their perception, they'd chased us here to the cemetery after watching us burst out of the shuttered Excited Ward, screaming and running for our lives. They must have thought we'd seen a ghost, and they weren't far off the mark.

To them, it was still the same day we had come to explore the asylum, searching for more clues about Emma and why her apparition continued to pursue us. But then, as we ran from the condemned ward into the cemetery, a shift had occurred and we woke up in restraints in The Hole.

I couldn't believe it. Our time in the asylum felt like months or more. But here we were again, back in the cemetery on the same day, maybe even the same moment that we had left.

I was sure our hysteria had been enough for Braden and Nick for an entire lifetime.

"Hey," Nick flinched as Emma brushed past him in haste. He reached for her arm, ready to hear some answers to her sudden appearance that might make sense.

The moment his fingers brushed against her sleeve, she jolted and spun around, swinging. Her closed fist connected with his jaw before he had time to dodge it.

"Get your grimy paws off me," she spat.

Nick's hand flew to his chin.

"Jesus," he groaned, rubbing his jaw. "She's crazy." He stared at her, struck at first by her undeniable beauty, but then his eyes narrowed in annoyance as she barreled away. "No, really. She's actually crazy."

I jumped toward him, ready to follow her.

"I'm so sorry, Nick." I checked his jaw for any redness. "She didn't mean it. She's just scared and confused right now. It's a long story."

Braden's gaze followed Emma as she moved farther from us.

"Can you guys just wait at the car for a couple seconds?" I asked Braden. "This is really important. Trust me. We know who she is, and we need to help her."

Braden's hesitation and furrowed brow made it clear he needed more information before leaving us.

Thinking fast, I added, "We need to bring her back. Tom will know what to do. We're just going to find him, and he'll help us."

Braden inhaled as if preparing his refusal.

"Tom disappeared," Nick interjected. "Again."

I glanced at him with narrow eyes as if he were nuts. But the truth was, he wasn't wrong. Tom seemed to come and go at the most random moments, leaving the guys confused. But I had a better understanding of him now and his role at the asylum. Tom had introduced himself as the groundskeeper of Blackwood, but I'd clarified his duty in my mind as simply *The Keeper*.

Braden moved closer and leaned in with a whisper. "Who the hell *is* she? She looks like she belongs locked in the wards."

A cough flew out of me as I choked on his comment. "I know. It's alright, though. She just needs our help. Okay? Meet us at the car?"

He nodded with reluctance and watched as we moved toward the woods after Emma.

"They must think we're out of our minds," Kaitlin whispered, looking back, sending a quick grin to Nick.

"Aren't we?" I murmured.

We scrambled to keep up with Emma. She swatted at branches and stumbled over logs, hurrying to get back to the asylum.

"I think it's this way." Emma pointed along a narrow trail. "You guys should go back now. Get out of here while you can before the security guards come searching for you."

We continued to follow close at her heels.

"Go," she repeated. "I need to get to Bobby. To let him know about their plan to murder us. He'll rage when he hears this. And won't Totten be surprised when she realizes we know the truth before she can make it happen."

My heart sank from her words.

She believed she was still in 1920, uncovering a conspiracy against our lives. Our gravestones convinced her that Totten planned to have us killed. Prescriptions for lobotomies or too much time in The Hole, it didn't matter how, only when. Her mission now was to stop it from happening--to take the control back.

We moved deeper along the trail and sunlight broke through the trees up ahead, along the border of the abandoned institution.

We were almost there, and my heart plummeted toward my feet in a panic.

She wasn't prepared to see the asylum in its current state of crumbling disrepair. She had to be warned that everything had changed, that everything she knew... was gone.

"Emma, stop!" I commanded. "There's something we need to tell you."

She continued to storm through the path, focused only on her mission of finding Bobby.

"Stop!" I froze on the trail, demanding her attention.

The sharp tone in my voice smacked her off the back of the head, and she twisted around with a scowl.

"What's your problem?" she seethed. "I thought you were running away. Go!" She swatted her hand at me. "You won't get a second chance."

Her words stung me, and I watched Kaitlin wince, as well.

This *was* our second chance--all of it. But now everything was in jeopardy. Emma was out of her time period and was too irrational to be reasoned with. She needed to be stopped so we could get back to our lives.

"Emma. Something's wrong. You need to listen." I struggled to hold her racing attention.

She glanced toward the direction of the asylum and then back at me. She studied my face, noticing the panic swirling in my eyes.

And then she ran.

"No, wait. Emma! Please!" We chased her through the trees. "Let me explain," I panted. "A lot of time has passed. Like a dream. A lot of time..."

We burst out of the woods into the clearing.

The grounds of the asylum opened up to us as the sun shone on the red brick buildings, illuminating the boarded-up doors and windows like a spotlight. The decrepit buildings glared back at us like sad, decomposing carcasses, as the deafening silence assaulted us from every direction.

As if suspended in eternal death, the stillness of the condemned grounds unsettled the deepest part of my being.

And then, as if a bomb detonated at our feet, the deathlike silence shattered.

A tortured scream ripped out of Emma as she exploded in frenzied disbelief. Covering her face with her hands, she pulled down on her eyes and took several steps closer, only to blink into the same vision of ruin.

A garbled groan of confusion and grief boiled out of her as she paced and wailed. Sickened by the sound of her anguish, I struggled to know what to say or do.

"Emma, please," I begged. "I can explain."

Fighting the urge to collapse, she ran closer to the buildings, panting, snapping her head toward each one in hopes of finding something she recognized. Something alive.

But it was all gone.

CHAPTER 2

Shuttered, condemned wards loomed around us with rotting woodwork over the entryways, peeling paint, and danger signs nailed to them. The old asylum was in fading ruin.

Emma lurched toward the chapel and shifted her stunned gaze up along the height of the clock tower. She gaped at the faded, handless clock face and then rotated robotically to us, trembling and twitching. Her face contorted in anguished grief twisting it into a visage of rage and revenge.

Panic coursed through me as I prepared myself for her next move. If there were ever a question of her sanity, now would be the moment of truth. Every irrational signal around her would be enough to trigger a meltdown of immense magnitude, and I was the target of her combustion.

Her eyes narrowed in stealth focus, and she launched at me in an explosive attack of screeching and clawing.

I cowered in defense, blocking her nails from ripping my face off, as venomous words spewed from her mouth crushing me in their agonizing accusations.

"What have you done? Evil bitches," she screamed. "Witchcraft? Trying to destroy me!"

The weight of her body flattened me on impact, toppling me to the ground. Before I could regain control, her hands knotted into my hair, ripping at it and smashing my head against the ground. Scattered stars glistened white in my field of vision as intense pain filled my skull.

"Get off her," Kaitlin shouted, tugging on Emma. "She has a head injury, you bitch!"

Kaitlin dragged Emma's flailing body off me, but not before she got a few last kicks into my ribs.

I groaned as I rolled onto my side, cradling my head in my arms.

"Stop!" Kaitlin yelled, squeezing tight around Emma. "We can explain everything if you give us a chance. But you have to calm down."

"Bobby!" Emma shrieked with a deafening blast. Her voice filled the dead space of the asylum grounds and bounced back to us in tortured anguish. "Where is he...?" The shrill pitch of her panicked voice mellowed into choking sobs. "What happened? I don't remember anything." She collapsed flat on her back with her arms outstretched, staring up into the sky. "Help me," she cried as tears streamed from her eyes, flowing into the grass beneath her.

I pushed myself up to sitting, running my hands through my hair, and took a moment to work through the dizziness in my skull. The sparkling stars had dissipated, but the searing pain behind my left eye remained. It didn't take much to aggravate my concussion symptoms, and a head slam to the ground was more than enough to bring them all back.

"Are you okay?" Kaitlin mouthed at me.

I nodded, pressing my lips together in annoyance. Emma always had to be the theatrical one, and this time I paid the price.

On all fours now, I crawled over to Kaitlin, and we hovered above Emma's splayed body. She cried with sickening moans, writhing in seething pain, as she attempted to process her desperate situation.

"Emma, you have to listen to us now," I said. "It's your only choice. You have to open your mind and hear what we are going to tell you. Okay?"

She rubbed her eyes and focused on my face, then dropped her head back again. "I can't do this," she mumbled, squeezing her eyes shut again. "Is Bobby dead?"

Her frightened words cut into my brain, alerting me to the source of her agony.

My breath sucked in with dread. I didn't have an answer for her angst-ridden question. It all depended on perspective. Did she mean now, in 2019? Did she mean in *her* 'now', 1920? I stuttered on the words that caught like cotton in my mouth.

"He, no, he... we don't know his situation right now," I chattered. "We need to explain it all to you first. It's about a weird time portal, Emma. I know it sounds impossible or nuts, but it's something to do with the power of the ward. It has a strange hold on us and..."

"I told you," she blurted, wiping tears off her face.

"What?" I pulled back.

"I told you it would never let go. It would have a hold on us forever." She closed her eyes and exhaled in frustration.

"Well, you were right then," I continued. "Emma, you've somehow landed in the future with us, the time where Kaitlin and I originally came from."

She sat up in an instant and stared at us. "What are you talking about? You've actually truly lost your marbles now." She huffed. "And I was crazy enough to think you were the sane one in our group." Her eyes narrowed, homing in on mine. "Stop trying to screw with me. It won't end well for you."

"Just look around," Kaitlin blasted. "You can see we're not crazy. The asylum's been boarded up for years. It's gone. Do you see the broken down buildings?"

"Do you think I can't see them?" Emma shouted. "I'm not blind. But it doesn't make sense what you're saying. None of it makes sense." Her hands pulled through her knotted hair. "It's a mind trick. You're just fucking with me."

I watched her confused torment as she scanned the condemned wards again. Her fingers tore at the fringed hem of her gray frock as she struggled to make sense of what she was seeing.

I searched for the right words to help explain better, the fewest amount possible in the quickest time.

"Emma. Kaitlin and I were in the cemetery one day and suddenly launched to the past, to the ward, with you. We found you in restraints in The Hole. Somehow, we were patients there, too. But that wasn't our current life. It was a strange past life." I started getting lost in my words again. "It's impossible to explain, but somehow we blasted back to our time, right now, and the thing is, you came too."

I stared at Kaitlin, begging for her to rescue me and come up with the right thing to say.

"We know it sounds crazy, but somehow, you returned to our future lives with us," Kaitlin continued. "Like, *you* entered the portal too."

"It makes sense in a way though," I added. "Because you had reached out to us, Emma. We saw an apparition of you. It was like you were reaching out for our help."

I paused, dropping my head back.

We sounded nuts. The right words just didn't exist for what we were trying to explain. There was only one thing that was clear and definite, though.

I cleared my throat. "We basically need to find a way to get you back to your time, Emma."

Emma remained silent, looking back and forth between us. With a long inhale, she wiped the grass off her frock. She stepped away from us and walked along the road that traversed along the front of the wards. Kaitlin and I followed her in silence, allowing her to process what she was seeing and hearing.

We passed without a sound along the front of the Quiet Ward and slowed as we reached the Excited Ward. Emma stopped in front of the entrance and stared at the crumbling stairs. Her eyes traveled up to the landing, studying the rotting woodwork of the entryway and then boring into the plywood board that blocked the door.

She swallowed hard and turned to us. "I always knew you two were from someplace... different. The words you used. The way you held yourselves. Modern." She looked us up and down. "Like you were from a different time. I suppose I always knew."

She looked down at her threadbare frock and then at our contemporary clothing with a huff.

"I mean, wearing your hose without a heavy skirt to hide your curves, it's rather risqué, wouldn't you say?" She waved a finger at my black leggings and lifted her eyebrows in feigned judgment. Then she sent a grin of approval, followed by a more severe glance. "None of it makes any sense. But I can see with my own eyes something strange has happened." She paused for a moment then glanced at me with somber eyes. "I'm sorry. I didn't mean to hurt you. It's just... a lot." She dropped her gaze to the ground.

Relief washed over me as she allowed the situation to percolate through her mind. Of course she would panic and become defensive in such a case. I was just grateful she was able to see it more rationally now.

"It's okay. I get it." I ignored my pounding head and watched as she moved through the numerous levels of understanding and acceptance.

"I don't care where I stay," she said with a shrug. "I don't care where I am. As long as I'm with Bobby. That's all that matters."

Kaitlin shot her wide eyes to mine in panicked alarm. My internal response sent the same level of urgency through me as well. Emma thought staying here with us was an option, as long as she found Bobby.

But Kaitlin and I were sure of one thing.

Emma could not stay here.

It was not an option.

Emma had to go back to her own time. It was the right thing to do, and there was no room for negotiation on that fact.

Kaitlin and I had saved her from killing herself. We'd accomplished what the asylum had reached out for us to do. Emma's ghost had called to us, pleading to help her.

And we did.

We'd stopped her at the hanging tree, just in time. We saved her life.

Or so we thought.

But now I wondered if we'd interfered too radically with fate.

We'd disrupted time somehow, and keeping Emma here could cause significant ripple effects through the cosmos with unknown extreme consequences. Having her here went against the laws of nature, and nature had a powerful way of showing her fury when crossed.

And plus, where would she go? Who would take care of her? She would clash with this modern world. I thought about it for another moment. Or maybe she would fit right in.

I always thought she was a modern thinker, ahead of her time. But, no. It would be wrong to transplant her like that. But it would be even worse to send her back to that hell hole we had been trapped in.

My inner thoughts battled in a war of right and wrong, good versus evil. And I was trapped in the middle--the one to decide.

I dropped my head back, staring up into the sky.

"Before anything else. Before anything is decided..." Emma interrupted my racing thoughts. "I need to get into the ward again, into the tunnels." She pointed to the entryway of the Excited Ward. "If there's any place we can find Bobby, it's in there."

CHAPTER 3

My body stiffened from her brusque words. Going back into the Excited Ward was the last thing on Earth I ever wanted to do. It had taken so much to break out, to escape it, and now she was suggesting walking right back in.

But the more I thought about it, the more it made sense.

The ward was powerful. It was the source of everything strange that had happened to us. And it had had the energy to pull us out of our current lives, into its confining restraints. Maybe it would pull Emma back in the same way.

I was sure the ward was part of the portal that caused the rift in our timelines, and Emma was right--it was worth searching for Bobby there too, or at least, more likely, for any clues of what became of him.

The obvious problem was clear, though. What if the power of the ward pulled Kaitlin and me back too? What if, this time, we couldn't get out--destined to be tortured patients in the madhouse, forever?

It could be a trap.

It may be the ward's way of sectioning us for good.

"I really don't want to go back in there." I squeezed my eyes shut, willing the moment away. But when I opened them, I still stared at the boarded door of the Excited Ward as it taunted me to re-enter.

"Me neither," Kaitlin whimpered. "I never want to go back in there, ever again."

The ward had left deep scars on our souls, ones that left us frozen in terror.

"We have to," Emma interjected. "It's the only way to figure this shit out. Straight from the evil source."

Her flippant tone made me stiffen, for fear the ward would pick on her disrespect, making matters worse.

A shudder ran up my spine. "What if we get trapped in there again? This time with no way out." My hands balled into fists.

"Braden and Nick know we're here," Kaitlin mumbled. "Maybe they can help if we need it."

I considered what Braden and Nick might be able to do to help us if we got caught in the ward, and beyond brawn, I didn't come up with much else.

"Yeah, but once we're in there, 'here' could be anywhere, any time." I looked toward the direction of where their car might be. "Once we're in there, Braden and Nick may not even exist anymore. We just don't know."

Kaitlin held my gaze as extreme worry poured from her eyes.

"You guys," Emma called out. "We don't have a choice. You need to help me. I don't care if it sends me back. I'll figure a way out. I need to find Bobby. Please."

I couldn't believe the entangled predicament we were in. It was like being trapped in a horror movie with no option but to go straight toward the killer's lair.

I turned back toward the direction of the car again, and then to Emma. Her desperation pulled at my gut, causing my teeth to grind.

"Shit," I spat, climbing the stairs to the boarded-up door. I tucked my fingers behind the plywood and pulled, searching for a weakness in the barrier. "Let's be fast before anything bad can happen."

Kaitlin scanned the grounds for any sign of witnesses, always feeling like a criminal, breaking and entering.

I prayed this would amount to a simple routine break-in of

condemned property. I could live with the legal consequences that would come from that type of activity.

It was the alternative that scared me more--the fear that something sinister lurked behind the sealed door, waiting for our return--waiting to reclaim our lost souls to a paranormal realm.

I chanted in my mind, "*It's okay. It's modern day. We're back safe.*" My self-talk continued. "*We just need to fix this little problem. This little... situation.*" The more I tried to soothe myself with unconvincing inner chat, the more I realized we were screwed.

Emma was here.

In our time.

How was that even possible?

The sincere hope that she would be absorbed back into the ward the moment we entered it sent hefty guilt through me. But it seemed like the best solution for all involved.

Emma had the tools to escape on her own when the time was right for her and Bobby. I had to believe that.

Her original plan, after Kaitlin and I had escaped, included her getting out with him and starting a new life in California, so it made sense to reset all of this for them.

It seemed possible.

Her gravestone had the same end date as ours, 1920.

It was the date of Kaitlin and my escape from the asylum. Maybe she escaped too, within the same year.

I strained to follow the possibilities in my mind but continued to land on one likely option. Emma escaped with us and never returned. She was here to stay.

My throat constricted at the thought. How would we manage her? In the eyes of our society, she didn't exist.

"Should we try the basement door around back?" Kaitlin glanced around the side of the ward. Her thoughts had likely raced along the same plane as mine, and she wasted no time trying to find a way to finish this.

Just as I considered her idea, my fingers moved deeper behind the board covering the front door, and it wobbled. A loose screw fell from the top corner, bounced at my feet, and rolled away.

Emma jumped and grabbed onto the board with me. "Oh my God. It's coming off." She yanked at the side of the plywood, and the screws along the edge popped out, one by one.

Before long, the entire side of the wood plank had broken free, and we were able to pry it open enough to see the dignified door hidden behind. Its tarnished brass knob beckoned us to turn it.

"Come on." I waved to Kaitlin. "We can squeeze in."

After one final hesitation, I reached for the knob and turned. With a pop, the door released from its hinges and shifted inward. I shimmied closer and pushed my shoulder into it. Emma pressed her weight against my back, and knocked me right into the musty foyer, falling into me as we burst inside.

Emma shifted her gaze as she steadied herself on her feet.

"It stinks." She blew air from her nose to clear it. Then she surveyed the decrepit condition of the ward, noting the peeling paint, mold stains on the chipping ceiling, and piles of rotting debris covering the floors. "I'm hoooome," she sang out.

Her voice traveled toward the back of the ward and faded without any reverberation.

"Huh," she sighed. "No welcome party?"

Kaitlin poked her head into the open doorway and snuck in behind us. "This is so creepy," she whispered. "It's so weird, after actually having been here when it was operational."

I couldn't agree more. No matter how old and deteriorated the place was, its pain remained raw.

Emma turned to us with a determined twinkle in her eye and then shot down the hallway.

She called back to us, "No time to waste. I'm going to find The Hole."

Before I could stop her, Emma bolted from the foyer, heading toward the back of the ward. My heart pounded in my ears as I followed her, half-expecting ghouls to pop out of every shadow or dark doorway and grab me.

A constant, evil nag twitched at the back of my brain, reminding me we were forever being watched in this place. I shook my head to clear the paranoia, only to return to the exact harrowing feeling of sinister control.

Totten.

I jumped with a skittish twitch as her name stabbed me between the eyes. Turning to Kaitlin for reassurance, I gasped from the look of terror that washed across her face.

"You feel it, too?" I choked.

She nodded with a grimace of resignation as if we were already dead before taking another step.

I closed my eyes in broken anguish. I never wanted to set eyes on that hateful witch again. I prayed she was long gone and turned to dust. But no matter how hard I wished her away, she was still there-- alive and strong in my mind, picking away at my last shreds of sanity.

I'd never be rid of Totten and the scars she left on my damaged soul. Her power over me, even still, clenched my jaw and balled my hands into tight fists.

"It's this way," Emma called back to us with excitement, barreling through the hallways.

It took every ounce of effort to get my muscles to move in her direction. My inner voice screamed to leave immediately, to get back outside to the safety of our known world.

But it was too late.

We were already here.

And now we had to see if crossing over again was even possible, for Emma's sake.

As the familiar dark alcove came into view, my nerves trembled. My breath burst in and out in a frenzy as my body tried resisting my approach toward the hidden door. The shameful secrets it concealed were haunting, tearing away pieces of my stability as I moved closer. Now, only raw terror remained.

"I don't want to go down there," Kaitlin whimpered.

Her terror matched mine, and its intensity caused a new shift within me—one of reason.

I had to face it.

If I ran, it would win.

Totten would win.

And I refused to allow that.

I had to face my fear and conquer it.

"It's just an old, broken-down building, Kaitlin. It doesn't control you anymore." I stepped closer to the door, next to Emma. "And don't forget, we survived it, Kaitlin. We won."

She remained fixed in her spot, staring at the ominous door. "Did we, though?"

Her haunting words settled deep in my bones. Her reluctance sent insecurity through me, but I fought it off with all my strength.

I'd felt the shift within me. I wasn't going to let the ward control me any longer, no matter how frightening it may be.

It was time to fight back.

"Well, I'm going down there," I said. "I need to see it. From a new perspective. One of freedom and power. Don't let it control you, Kaitlin. Come on."

I pulled on the door, and it stuck solid. Emma reached her hands around mine, and we tugged together. Inch by inch, the swollen wooden door creaked out of its warped position within its rotting frame.

"Harder," Emma blasted. "It's almost free."

And with her final syllable, the door released and flew open, sending us hurtling back.

Kaitlin launched forward, steadying us before we fell. Then she stepped past us to the fateful opening and peered into the darkness. Emma and I hovered over her shoulder and stared with her into the eerie abyss.

Moldy, stale air wafted up and coated our faces with its stench, making us cough. It was no different from the time we'd spent down there in restraints. The cold, damp cellar stood stagnant, awaiting its next victims.

"Me first," Emma stated with flat affect, as she pushed out of our huddle.

My heart stopped at the thought of going down there, but before I could consider any alternative, she was gone.

Holding the sidewall, she stepped cautiously onto each stone stair, feeling ahead with her foot for the next one. Reluctantly, we followed into the lonesome darkness, waiting for our eyes to adjust to the low light that pooled in from behind us.

As we landed onto the solid dirt floor, we moved along the narrow space, passing the first closed door on the right. Without a word, we continued toward the second door, knowing well it was the gateway to The Hole.

"This is so crazy," Emma whispered. "I'd usually be screaming and struggling at this point, looking for any opportunity to gouge out the eyes of whoever was demented enough to bring me down here." She inhaled and held it for a moment. "It's my first time coming here by choice." She chuckled. "Weird."

I huffed, remembering the horrors of being trapped down here, tied to a metal table, freezing. Unlike Emma, I couldn't find any humor in the situation.

She moved forward and reached for the door handle. "Ready?" She turned to be sure we were with her, then pushed.

"Jesus Christ," Emma blasted, stepping into the cold room. "It's exactly the same as the day we left it."

I pressed in behind her for a look around. Light filtered in through the gaps in the boards that covered the small, lead glass window at the top of the back wall. My eyes widened as I pulled in every intimate detail of the miserable room.

Metal tables stood in the middle with cracked leather restraints hanging from the sides--the buckles of the straps lay on the ground, rusting. A rickety table stood at the front of the room holding metal trays and dented tin bowls.

"It's still here," Emma called out, leaning over one of the tables. "What's left of it, anyway."

I moved in behind her and looked over her shoulder. Laying across the table, strapped into place, was an old-fashioned, disintegrating peacoat, displaying its fancy brass buttons with pride.

"It's Betty's," I whispered. "I guess she never got to wear it again." A lump formed in my throat, making it difficult to swallow.

I wondered whatever became of Betty. The kindness in her heart saved every girl in the ward at one time or another. I'd never know if she ever got out, but maybe she wasn't meant to.

"It's exactly how I left it," Emma stated. "No one's been in here since us."

Kaitlin stepped closer and inspected the coat. "Didn't the superintendent say they'd close it off, never to be used again?"

I shot my eyes to Kaitlin. Her memory was so clear, and her words jarred my own memories of our final moments at the ward.

"You're right," I said. "Dr... Dr. Johnson. I can't believe you remember that, Kaitlin. What else do you remember?"

She swallowed hard.

"It's coming back to me in floods down here. Faces, voices, feelings. Do you feel it, too?" She stared at me with wide eyes.

Everything was still hazy for me. It always floated away just as I tried to grasp any details.

I shook my head. "No. Not like that. It's all still a blur."

She squinted her eyes. "Well, I can't seem to stop it." Her head dropped back like she was trying to resist. "It's like a movie that keeps playing in my mind, a horror movie."

I watched her face turn three shades of green. "Are you okay? You look like you're going to be sick."

Her throat squeaked as she swallowed hard.

"I need to get out of here." She stumbled to the door and fell out into the corridor, gasping for air. "Please, it's all too vivid. Like she's here, all around us. I need to go."

It didn't take a genius to know who she was talking about. And now that she mentioned it, I had to admit, I felt her here, too. Everywhere. Her wicked soul remained trapped in this place, right where it belonged. And getting as far away from it as possible was the absolute priority.

I grabbed onto Emma and tugged her away from the table and the coat. "Come on. Let's get out of here. Totten's ghost is all over this place."

She resisted my pull, hanging onto the side of the table with one hand and the arm of the coat with the other. Her eyes blazed with hatred as if she were reliving her torture in The Hole.

I pulled harder and broke her away from the table.

"You're free now, Emma." I yanked her toward the door. "You have to let it go, knowing nobody else will ever be trapped in here again."

"I can't," she blasted. "They hurt me. They hurt us." Tears fell from her eyes. "I can't ever forget. And now, now they're still winning. Look at us! Damaged goods and their claw marks are all over us." She shot her eyes out the door with a panicked stare and then barreled toward it. "If Totten's still here, then bring her to me!"

She threw herself toward the stone stairs and flew up them, tripping, taking two stairs at a time.

"That bitch can't control me ever again!" She shrieked. "I make my rules now, and I'll see who I want to see."

Kaitlin and I chased her up the stairs.

"Bobby," she screamed as she raced out of the cellar. "Bobby!"

Kaitlin and I ran after her as she bombed through the corridor toward the stairwell at the back of the ward. Without hesitation, she pulled the loose cross-boards away, tripped over a 'Not an Exit' sign, and jumped onto the stairs.

With thumping steps, we bounded down the crumbling stairwell. Red paint letters smeared across the wall in old messy graffiti. The words 'Help Us!' shot out at me as we flew past the scrawl and then the word, 'Run!' raised my fear to terror levels as I fell into the basement hallway.

We stopped, breathless, and peered into the dark corridor. Chunks of rotted ceiling hung from wires above and water pooled in damp areas across the tiled floor. Then, at the same time, we all turned to the dim corner behind us--the obscure location of the secret door to the tunnels.

Emma raced to the rusted, metal door and gripped the handle. She heaved on it with all of her strength, but it didn't budge. I searched the piles of debris around us and pulled a broken mop pole out of a mound of trash. Jamming the snapped end into the side of the door, I pushed on it like a wedge.

"Pull again," I commanded Emma.

And together, I pushed on the pole while she pulled on the door. Kaitlin jumped in and struggled with us. Then, with a crunch of releasing corroded metal, the door broke free from its rusted seal.

We froze, staring at each other, too terrified to make another move.

The door was open only slightly, with the smallest crack, but it offered a world of daunting potential to us.

Before we could make another move, a hollow echo escaped through the narrow opening and whirled around us like a curious ghost. Our ears twitched, and we moved closer to hear it better.

Then Emma stood rigid.

"Bobby?" She pressed her ear into the opening and then screamed, "It's Bobby!"

If you are ready for Book Three, be sure to grab a copy of The Forgotten Ward.

CHAPTER 4

Before we could stop her, she heaved the door open enough to squeeze in and was gone. Emma bolted blindly through the darkness of the tunnels, screaming Bobby's name.

"No! Emma, wait for us," I shouted into the thick gloom. "What do we do?" I turned to Kaitlin. "We can't just follow her aimlessly!"

She fumbled in her empty pockets. "Do you have your phone?" Kaitlin squinted into the darkness, waiting for my reply.

I checked the pocket of my hoodie, holding my breath, and wrapped my fingers around it with hopeful anticipation. Pulling it out, I pressed the side button, praying it would come to life.

"Thank God," Kaitlin exhaled.

"It's at twelve percent. Let's go!" I swiped my flashlight on and shone it down through the dark tunnel. "We don't have much time."

Kaitlin held the back of my sweatshirt as we ran into the cold, dank passageway. "We can't go too far. Your battery will drain fast," she pleaded.

She knew too well that twelve percent on my phone meant more like two percent. We had about five minutes max in flashlight mode.

"We'll follow the white pipes. If we need to, we can feel our way back." I reached up to be sure I could touch them, and my fingertips brushed along their rough, chipping surface. "Emma!" I shouted into the darkness.

Deep within the tunnels, her voice resonated in the depths of the twisting maze.

"That way," Kaitlin pointed toward the loudest sound.

"The pipes don't go that way." I raised my light to the ceiling to show her. "It's too risky."

We hovered, breathless, trying to decide what to do.

"Bobby!" Emma's voice shot straight at us from the darkness.

"She's close!" I turned in the new direction, and we raced along the narrow passage, slipping on wet patches under our feet. "Emma, wait!"

We stumbled along, choking on the musty air, as we called her name. Emma's muffled echoes became more evident as we moved deeper into the labyrinth of twists and turns.

Panic coursed through my veins as I realized we were being lured further into the heart of the tunnels. My feet slowed as I considered the random turns we'd taken to get to this point. I'd already lost my way without the bread crumb trail of the white pipes.

"Grace! Kaitlin!" she called to us. "Hurry! I hear him."

Kaitlin pushed on my back to get me moving again. "Go, go, go..."

We raced toward the sound of Emma's muddled voice, and as we turned the next corner, we smacked right into her. My arms flew around her shoulders, and I held on for dear life.

"Jesus! Don't leave us again," I panted. "You could've been lost in here. Forever. We need to stick together."

Then my ears perked up, focusing on a sound from deep within the tunnels.

"Emma..." The harrowing voice made the hairs on the back of my neck stand up as it searched in desperation.

"Do you hear it?" Emma blasted. "It's him! I know it is. It's Bobby!"

Unblinking, I strained to listen for it again. The sound of my heart pounding in my ears threatened my ability to hear correctly.

"Emma..." The lost sound of the voice shot me straight in the heart.

I didn't want to admit it. Every bone in my body attempted to reject the roar. But it was impossible. His voice echoed from deep within.

"I hear it," I whispered.

She sucked in a sharp, disbelieving inhale. "I knew it! Come on," Emma shrieked. "We have to follow it!"

She pulled on my sleeve, and we raced along with her, stumbling through every erratic stride.

"We're getting farther away from the ward," Kaitlin warned. "We won't be able to find our way back."

She confirmed the worry that nagged at my soul. Becoming lost down here in the pitch dark would be the most horrifying experience that I hoped never to have to encounter.

I checked my phone--eight percent and draining faster now.

"Emma..." The desperate cries echoed all around us, making it impossible to choose the right direction.

"Bobby!" Emma's voice cracked with strain. "Follow my voice!"

She turned along a wider section of the tunnels, and we gathered in behind her. I lifted my light and pointed it along the sidewall, illuminating a large wooden door. A white sign hung crooked off the middle, with some of the black letters corroded and worn off.

I sounded out the words as best I could. "... RAIN ...BAN."

Without hesitation, Emma pushed the door open, and we spilled inside.

"Bobby," she called out. "Are you in here?"

I shot my light beam in every direction, searching for any sign of him, only to find a vast space lined with multiple shelves along the walls. Rows of large glass jars covered every shelf, and we moved closer to inspect their contents.

My flashlight passed over another sign at the far side of the chamber, and as the words processed through my mind, the contents of the glass jars became clear. Suspended in yellow liquid, squiggly masses floated in each container, well preserved against the pressure of time.

Kaitlin read aloud, "Brain Bank," freezing on the last sound as it left her mouth. "What the hell is that?" She choked as her voice trailed off into a drawn-out sound while she stared knowingly at the jars.

Mouth agape, I stepped back, overwhelmed by the sheer amount of glass containers, each holding a perfectly preserved brain floating in formaldehyde.

I couldn't imagine what they would need so many brain specimens for. Research? Testing? And what the hell were they doing down here, stored secretively? My head shook as I considered the harvesting, most likely done without donor consent.

"Oh. My. God." Emma sauntered along the shelves, trailing her fingers across a row of jars." "So this is what they do with us." She giggled. "Psychos."

Just as her last syllable cut into my head, my light died, leaving us in complete darkness.

A thick blanket of darkness bore down on us, and we huddled together. Only our rapid breathing was heard from our frozen stance within the terrifying blackened room of jarred brains.

Then our breathing stopped short, and we listened in stealth silence. Our nails dug into each other's arms as a haunting sound of clomping footsteps resounded in from the tunnels, growing louder with every step.

I gasped in terror as the sound drew nearer.

"What the fuck is that?" Kaitlin whimpered.

Our breath turned to pants as dread rose in us. The inability to move kept us locked in our stance as we waited for the coming of our doom. Terror caused tears to spill from my eyes as I stared without blinking into the darkness.

Then the sound stopped, leaving us in the mounting fear of our shuddering circle.

"We need to get out here." Kaitlin pulled us in the direction of the door. "We can't stay here, trapped, or she'll find us."

Her words sent panic through me. Speaking the idea of someone being out there, coming for us, was more than I could handle. And being cornered like skittish quarry was even worse.

"Shut up," I seethed. "No one's out there. It's impossible."

Emma rubbed her hand on my arm. "Don't be so sure, love. Anything's possible down here. You should know that."

I held my breath again, listening with every fiber of my being.

"Stop it." I pulled my arm away from her. "If you believe that, you'll *make* it happen. You'll jinx it."

"What the hell does that mean?" She whispered through clenched teeth. "You don't actually think..."

Then another clomp, closer this time.

My heart stopped as I stared wildly into the blackness.

"What is that?" Kaitlin screamed in panic, digging her nails deeper into my arm. "We need to leave!"

Her screeching voice pierced through my skull, causing my eyes to squint.

"Silence!" A voice burst through the door filling the space around. "Or you'll remain in The Hole another week!"

Her voice knocked the wind out of me as if being punched in the gut. My bones unhinged in terror, making it near impossible to move. Kaitlin and Emma yanked me, knocking me out of my paralysis, and before another moment passed, we barreled toward the door.

Jars rattled as we banged against the shelving, searching for our escape. I ran my hands along the wall, feeling for any sign of the exit while Emma and Kaitlin clawed at the surface as if trying to dig their way out.

"Here," Emma called out. "The door!"

She yanked it open, and we fell out into the passageway, tumbling over each other in the direction we had come. Tripping on the uneven terrain, keeping our hands running along the walls, we felt our way through the shrouded path of the nightmarish tunnel, wondering if we'd be attacked from the dark at any moment.

"It turns here," Emma gasped.

"Here, too." Kaitlin tugged in the opposite direction.

I couldn't remember which way we had come, and the desperate panic had me completely turned around.

"Which way should we go?" Emma begged.

More clomping echoed from the depths of blackness to our left, and my mind exploded in terror. We grabbed each other again and sprang for the turn in the opposite direction.

Tripping through the narrow passage, we moved blindly, each one trying to get ahead of the other for fear of being grabbed from behind.

"Wait. I hear something," Emma whispered, slowing.

"Don't stop," Kaitlin cried, pushing her along.

"No, wait," she hesitated. "Hear that?"

A sound from far ahead rolled past our ears, halting our erratic breathing to silence.

"Emma..." The grieving voice echoed through the tunnels.

With the evil footsteps of Totten behind us, I didn't hesitate for a moment on the decision to follow the beacon of his voice.

"I hear it. Let's go," I blasted, pushing on them. "Go, go, go!"

I shouldered the others ahead of me, shoving them to move faster, certain Totten would grab me any moment to pull me into oblivion. I was sure I felt her foul, hot breath on the back of my neck.

"Emma..." The harrowing sound of the voice pulled us through the darkness.

And then, BANG.

Emma smashed into a metal blockade sending a loud boom reverberating through the maze behind us.

"What is it?" I said, pushing my way through them.

I felt the rusting surface of the metal and pushed my hands all over it. At the edge, my fingers moved onto a seam and trailed up, finding a hinge.

"Hurry! What is it?" Kaitlin pressed up behind me.

I continued to search until I found it.

A handle.

"It's a door. Help me pull."

I cracked the lever handle downward and yanked.

"Grab at my hands," I said. "Tug, hard."

The three of us secured strong holds on the lever, and as we readied to pull at the same time, a sound trailed up behind us.

"Not so fast, missies." The vile sound hissed at us, sending adrenaline to every muscle and we heaved.

My heart pounded, knowing we were caught. She'd reached us, and the terror of her grasp caused me to pull even harder.

The door crunched and then opened a crack, sending a nerve-wracking groan through the darkness that could wake the dead. But immediately following the booming sound was a beam of lifesaving sunlight.

The light of day poured into the tunnel as we pulled the door further open and sprang for it.

Clambering over one another, we fell out of the tunnel, pulling our feet out before being sucked back in by the evil forces that tormented us.

I stared back into the gaping darkness of the tunnel, waiting for any sudden movement or eerie sound. After a moment, with a massive shudder of relief, I jumped to the door and pulled it shut with a smash.

∽

"Jesus Christ," Kaitlin exhaled with trembling breath.

We climbed up the cement stairs that led to ground level. I looked back down to the door and continued to move further away for fear of it bursting open again with Totten's corpse launching out for us.

"I can't believe we got out of there," I murmured.

If we hadn't stumbled upon the metal door, it was terrifying to think what might have happened. My mind ran in every horrifying direction of being trapped in there forever, tortured by Totten, always searching for a way to escape--stuck in the asylum's evil limbo for all eternity.

With a vast exhale, my shoulders dropped from my ears, and I glanced around at our new location. In surprise, my eyes ran up the full height of high chain link fencing that surrounded us. I checked every direction, only to find ourselves imprisoned within a high-security perimeter. Trapped.

"What is this place?" Kaitlin murmured, examining the tight-linked fencing. "It feels like we're in a huge cage."

Emma took a step toward the boarded-up building behind us, confined within the fencing as well. She glanced at the front entry and then looked up toward a second-story window on the right side.

With a sinister grin, she said, "The ward for the criminally insane." And then with a chuckle, added, "It's Ward B."

Made in United States
Troutdale, OR
10/10/2025

40060942R10132